Letters

From

Abroad

The Past Lives on...

A novel by Charles Andrews

ISBN: 9798642436813

For John Charles Sparrowhawk

1965-2017

A mentor, hero, friend and uncle.

Contents

Prologue

You may call me Sven.

This is the story of two people I used to know, from my days as a student at Princeton. This was where I first met Brian, my former housemate and fellow travel companion.

The other was a university lecturer who taught English literature; a rare sight for a woman to be leading a faculty. Cassandra.

It was the mid 1930s.

The years of University life ended, as all things must; the passing of time cannot be stopped; it is like the summer into the autumn.

Brian moved to Indochina as a journalist before returning to London on the brink of war. Cassandra went to the state of California to work for the San Francisco Chronicle. One of them was chasing their dream, the other dealt with a career restructure against their desires. They never spoke to each other again after their time in university, yet they both often did, to me.

They both wrote to me detailing their lives and what they had decided to do with their time now that they were outside of the university life. He was a dreamer, who wandered the world looking for things that he could enjoy. She was callous, ambitious and manipulative, although not without being funny, brave and inspiring.

I was always the third person with their friendship. I knew all that happened within the grounds of Princeton because they both confided in me. But whilst I always respected her, I saw through her ploy to cause dramas. All of this will be revealed in time. All the letters they sent me, all the notes and all the confessions found their way into my desk in Lisbon and later Stockholm one by one over the years.

Yes, I replied to them, but I never encouraged them to speak to each other. I had no need – they were better outside of each other's lives. I saw them move on, grow, develop and actually turn into pretty decent people. They seemed to be doing quite well.

I physically never saw either of them again after I left Princeton. They went to live different lives and so did I. Then fascism rose up in Europe and cut off the mainland from the United Kingdom. The United Kingdom was cut off from America. America was cut off from us. The letters we exchanged gradually slowed down, the replies I could give offered no information about my country for reasons of national security. I could only reply to them. Yet my 'involvement' in matters concerning their current paths in life left me with little I could say.

But never did we truly lose touch.

Slowly, contact was re-established after the fall of Fascism in Europe. And yet my replies on my own situation were largely muted – interest in how they were living their lives was all that lingered on. I held no focus on my own life; after all I had a family to support, otherwise doing very little other than managing my career as a civil servant in Stockholm. We moved back from Lisbon in the late 1940s. Actually, there is not much of interest in my life I can add. A career as a civil servant has left me rather dull and uninspiring.

But it also never occurred to me, over forty years ago, to ever save a copy of the letters that I sent to them. It was merely rambling to each other, as one does with someone one Thursday morning when you prepare for the mountain of work that you know awaits you in the office. Thus, my own exchanges with them are locked away in my memory. There they shall remain.

Yet the separate lives that these two individuals have left behind *are* inspiring. It has been almost forty years since the final letters were exchanged and I face the twilight of my own apathetic existence in the world. I am coming to the end of my life and with that, thus this story shall whither and die, like the last defiant plants in the November frost.

Within these pages stand the notes and letters left behind of these two people I once shared time, space, emotional and physical energy with. These are *their* stories, not mine. I am merely the historian who can tell the tale. It is not their only legacy – it is the legacy of a time gone by when things were very different and people lived in a way that we now may not understand.

I have deliberately used fictional names as history may judge these two harsher than their actions in these letters would deem fair. Things that have happened in these letters are true – I shall not tell you how I can know all of this for sure, because I do not. Only that both of them never shared anything with me that I had previously considered a lie. I do not see why things would ever change.

My own name shall remain a mystery to all. It is my duty to tell their story before there is no one else left to do so and it is lost in the currents of time's river. It is not my right to discredit them or to embarrass whoever might be left behind from their blood line. This is why you shall never know my true name. To the best of my knowledge, all these letters that you read are in chronological order, starting back in 1936 and ending by 1950. In our current year of the lord, that would place me at the age of seventy-seven.

I show you these letters, not only to offer you some insight into their lives as people, but for my own catharsis. Their lives and stories are not ones I wish to take to the grave; they are a shared past that ties in with my own. I wish to offer them a chance to be judged fairly by the more liberal present than the conservative past that they both actively rebelled against through their excessive drinking, hedonism and zealous lust for life. And perhaps in that, we can all find some redemption.

Our story starts in 1935. These letters are somewhat scattered; dates have been lost by coffee spills or simple carelessness on my part. I have tried to piece the story together, date by date until the final page and the last marks on ink. I hope you agree with me when I say I have done my best to represent them to you as they were.

The last thing I want you to remember as you turn these pages, reading about the mistakes he made, the actions she committed in order to survive and the life I breathe back into them all these years later is this. That no matter what you judge, feel, applaud in or despise – it is all true. Names are altered, yes. But dates, times, locations, events, the prose and the tone of these pages. Those are real. None of it has ever been changed. I was there for some of it.

Every word is true.

And may I welcome you back to 1935.

Part I

April 1936
University of Princeton

Dear Sven,

Had to dash out this morning to get an essay in on time. Screwed the dates up and thought it was for tomorrow. Borrowed your bike. Tried to wake you to ask your permission but frankly you were out cold from the obscenely late night you pulled trying to get your own stuff done. Really hope you don't mind but I was left with no alternative. I cannot afford to flunk my degree.

See you when I'm back,

Yours

Brian

July 1936
University of Princeton

Dear Sven,

Hungover much? Just heading out to see a friend for coffee but do you want to meet this evening? I'll be in the Chaucer student bar by around 7 so you know where to find me?

That Cassandra is a pretty good looking girl, isn't she?

We both seem to get on with her pretty well – I would love to spend another hour discussing literature with her. Did you know she teaches here? I did not realise until she mentioned that she was supervising a couple of students on PHDs. I mean, she cannot be that old? I don't know how old she is but she's really stunning. Taken care of herself and makes it attractive to be a lecturer here.

I actually find her a bit attractive in a weird way. She's got this charisma to her that makes her appealing. You should have introduced me to her sooner – do you think we could meet up with her again sometime?

See you at the bar,

Brian.

September 1936
University of Princeton

Dear Sven,

I'm so glad you have enjoyed the summer, travelling around New England. The landscape is stunning – what did you like best about Maine? I grew up there. How was Brian on the trip? I'd like to talk to him about his literature thesis. When we spoke a few days ago in the bar, he told me about his interest in authors of modernism. Happens to be something that I specialise in.

I'd be interested in helping him develop his ideas. He's a bit of a typical student, talking about his grand ideas and flirting with girls but there is something pretty alluring about him.

Anyway, do you fancy meeting later in the week? Few things to tell you about the coming semester.

See you later

Cassandra

November 1936
University of Princeton

Hey Sven,

Haven't seen you for a few days.

Got a few updates.

Broke it off with that girl I was sleeping with in September. She put out and wasn't bad to go to bed with. Just not my type in the end.

Decided to take up football or soccer as the yanks call it on campus. I'm centre mid-field. It's a bit of fun and helps me keep fit.

Speaking of keeping fit, started smoking again. Just too tempting.

Oh and I met Cassandra in her office the other day. She's offered to supervise my project for my final year. The deadline is due just before May starts. Not sure what I'll write in on yet but she seems to think I can come up with something.

Want to go to a bike ride this weekend?

Brian

December 1936
University of Princeton

Hey Sven,

Going to be off Campus for the Christmas break in New York.
Seeing some friends. Do you want to join us for the New Years
Eve party? You can reach me at my family address in Brooklyn.

Oh and do not bring Brian if you can help it. In addition to him
needing to put down the wine glass and hit the books for his
thesis; I find him strangely alluring and could do without the
temptation. It's been a while since I've had sex and I don't want to
run into any risky issues. Like sleeping with a student simply
because he is attracted to me. I have seen the way he looks at me.

Hope to see you at the party,

Cassandra

February 1937
University of Princeton

Hey Sven,

Just a note to tell you that I'll be at Cassandra's house all evening, off campus. She's tutoring me on my thesis. I mean, it all seems business like. She tells me I need to get my act together or I run the risk of flunking my degree.

So I've agreed to it. I actually love being around her. She is pretty attractive and I find her intelligence to be profound. She seems to know so much on the realm of literature and has given me numerous books to help with my work.

During our time together, she reads my work and tells me what I need to improve. We occasionally share dinner and a glass of wine together. I really like this part because she treats me as an equal in these moments; not as a student. So I'm going to continue seeing her for now.

I fantasize about sleeping with her and flirt with her, although she seems to put off these advances by reminding me that I'm her student. That some would frown on us spending time together outside of university hours; she assures me it is for the greater good as I need the tuition to get a better degree. That it can remain between us. I'm only really telling you because I imagine she's told you by now.

Anyway, see you later.

Brian

April 1937
University of Princeton

Dear Sven,

I've done something fucking stupid.

Slept with Brian. More than once I should add.

He came onto me. The first time. We were on the sofa, talking and laughing. We had become closer over the last few months; being around each other a lot lately. Anyway, he moved to kiss me on the check to thank me for something that I'd said and I turned my mouth to his and intercepted the kiss on the cheek to my mouth.

We fell on each other on the floor and had sex. The odd thing about it was that it did not seem strange afterwards. He cuddled up to me as we lay naked on the floor. I smoked a cigarette and offered him one as we lay there. In those moments, I thought to myself and realised that he was totally into me. Not the other way round. That he started this, although I did not refuse him because I knew he wanted me and that it felt good to be seen as attractive by a younger person.

We've met up several times since then. We originally agreed that it had been fun but that we needed to keep it professional. This lasted about ten minutes when we went into my bedroom and made love. We then had sex a second time and then he stayed in my bed before sneaking off early in the morning at my recommendation.

And then there has been two more occasions. I know I'm putting my career at risk but honestly I enjoy his body. I'm an older, unmarried woman. I do know that he keeps coming back for more because he is attracted to me as a person. I just sleep with him because he is a good fuck and knows how to pleasure a woman.

Once he finishes his semester, he will probably return to England. I know that his visa will expire upon the end of the semester and that this will not last. I'll end up breaking the boy's heart, I know that much. He definitely likes me more than I like him.

Oh, I'm an idiot for doing this but he comes over again tonight. The fourth time in the last two weeks. You've probably wondered why he keeps disappearing. Well, it's to see me. And I keep encouraging it because I like the sex.

This will end my career if word gets out, so I'm asking you for help. Help me let him down slowly so that nothing happens to him. Or me.

Cassandra

May 1937
University of Princeton

Dear Sven,

I have left this letter for you in hopes that you discover it and that we can maintain contact. Since we've both been so busy lately, I've hardly had the time to tell you about everything that has been going on.

To start with, I'm moving to Saigon and this is confirmed. Contract signed, apartment sorted on a six month lease whilst I sort out a long term plan and passage to Saigon booked. I go back to England for about three weeks to sort out affairs there and then I shall be leaving shortly after. This has always been a plan of mine; it is time to act upon it.

I handed my final thesis in and finished my last exam four days ago. I am leaving the flat that we've rented this last semester in about three hours and will be making my way to New York, where I shall take a boat to head to Portsmouth in England. After that, a train and a car ride to my father's house in Hampshire. It'll be a long few days and plenty of time to dig my nose into the books.

What happened with Cassandra, the woman I was with on this final semester that kept me so busy and so secretive?

She broke it off with me. We both knew it was not going to last. But I stupidly developed feelings for her and when it came to breaking it off, she was ruthless. Like a business woman and not an advocate of the arts who gives so much of her time to the field of understanding love. It was cold and calculated and has left me feeling empty. It was not like it was a one night stand or anything.

We'd been sleeping together for months. She'd encouraged me to come to her flat to help me with my work. Additional tuition was the phrasing she'd used. When we first slept together it was on the floor of her living room. It did not happen overnight, despite my attractions to her. It was on our forth or fifth study session, after the attraction I held towards her had time to register in her mind. In many ways, I think she was fully aware of my attraction to her from the off. And I think she used it completely for her own ends.

She told me in the beginning how we were just sleeping together and if I told anyone she'd ensure I was sent home on the next boat without my degree. It was essentially emotional blackmail. I saw her as a conquest. I've always liked the girls. Her intellect was her selling point. That and even you would admit that a woman of her figure doesn't look bad for her age.

But anyway…it's over now. She basically told me it had to end. She told me to keep in touch but honestly no. No. I'm cutting her off. For my own good. She'll never hear from me again. My adventure on the east coast ends in heart ache and regret.

So I'm leaving for Saigon by way of England and I'll be out there for at least six months. I feel directionless. Like my studies culminated into the fall of the boy and the birth of the man. She told me that I'm far from a man yet but that I am becoming a man soon enough. We will see. I would not go so far to say that she forced herself on me in the beginning but the truth is that I had no concept on how to handle an older woman. Her experience and skill made me realise as I lay between her legs that all my shameless affairs with women over the years could not prepare me for the heartache to follow. I was undoubtedly more keen on keeping things long term than she was. To her, I was fun. The student who idolised the master and fell for her charms.

And now I feel broken and used. Still a boy, not really a man at all. This is simply something I cannot shake. I do not want to know about her for now.

I just want to be left alone and to move on with my life.

Stay in touch Sven,

Brian.

July 1937
Saigon

Dear Sven,

I've been in Saigon for almost three weeks or so now. Securing a job as a junior journalist was easy enough, thanks to the contacts at the university and my father. I live in this old house roughly twenty minutes from work. It is run by this tiny woman called Phong, who could be forty or sixty – it becomes hard to tell the age of natives in this country. She doesn't speak any English but we get by through broken French.

I like it here but it is too early to say how long this will last. It is a world apart from what we knew in America. But the land is awe-inspiring and the history of this country absolutely fascinates me. The French have truly dug their heels into the soil but the Vietnamese, at least to me, seem to live side by side with their white counter-parts.

But I'm not really writing this letter to tell you about Indochina. You know I'd just tell you to read a book on the country.

No, I'm writing to talk to you about Cassandra. I have not spoken to her since we finished. I do not know if I want to for a long time. This is one of the reasons why I became so insistent that I left for Saigon. What I really want to say is that for the first time in my life, I feel like a man and I suppose a part of that is owed to her association with me. I cannot say I want to forgive her nor do I want to know her anymore. She has hurt me and created ripples that cannot be halted over night.

Instead, what I'm writing to say is that I know you and her have a friendship that existed outside of my feelings for her. That the two of you are friends. So I want you to know that I am willing to honour your mutual relationship of each other – but I do not want to know her. So if you choose to converse with her then it is fine by me. But there is no reason for me to know about it. I respect you Sven and I like you. But I do not want to have to discuss her in my letters. Not for a long time at least.

Sven, I'll be in Saigon for a while. You can reach me at my office for letters; you can write to me at anytime and talk to me about things. Just do not mention Cassandra unless you really feel the need to do so – I do not need to know about her anymore. The time has come to move on. I care not for her. But I care for you and I support your right to be friends with her. But I don't want to know about her.

Enjoy the Swedish summers my friend. It has done little but rain over here and by the time you read this letter it will have rained more. I sit in a café, opposite the *Basilique-Cathedrale Notre-Dame*, smoking and drinking coffee whilst I wait for the day to begin. The city is full of life and I actually think I'm going to enjoy my time here.

Sven, know that I love and respect you. I will be in contact here and there while I find my feet in this city. Be well my friend,

Brian

November 1937

New York

Dear Sven,

Well, I've fucked it, haven't I?

I cannot get a teaching job anywhere. No one will hire me. I'm not sure if it is because I am a woman, the employment in America being dire because of the 'Great Depression' or because Princeton have blacklisted my name. Knowing those dry old men – the latter.

I was told in July, just after the last of the students left, to go to the Deans office. He sternly told me that they knew what I was 'up to' and that I had a choice. They could either let me go and leave it at that or fire me and report me to the police for my actions. I had no choice. People probably saw us. Someone said something. I could not deny that I had broken the law but I simply told them I'd go. I do wonder if there was ever a political motivation for this – I was not on the best of terms with many of the staff and preferred the students. Like someone was looking for an excuse.

I guess it does not matter now.

I'm staying in New York City right now. I love the city and it feel safe here but if I cannot get a job here then what good am I? Right now, I work as a private assistant for a company that deals in fashion on Madison Avenue. Let me tell you that it sucks, although I can at least put food on the table.

I guess Brian told you what happened? Truth be told, it was not just me at fault. He fucked me too Sven. A lot. He is an adult and needs to recognise his actions. Mine have cost me my career – whilst he is young and fresh enough to go on in life.

I'm suffering from pretty bad mood swings right now. I feel like I need a fresh start in life. I think moving might be a good idea. Another city maybe.

I know Brian is your friend but we are friends too. I'm grateful that you haven't taken sides in this – that you have honoured our friendship. I'd do the same for you Sven. I'm sorry about the situation with him but we must preserve our friendship.

Yours my friend,

Cassandra

March 1938

New York

Dear Sven,

So I'm moving to San Francisco! I'm aware that lately things have been quiet on my end. I'll quickly explain since I am in a hurry to pack – I leave tomorrow on a plane.

To start with, I had dinner with a friend of my late father's last month, Ross. We spoke about the problems I've faced and my issues with not having a decent career anymore. He was empathetic. He told me that whilst it is unfortunate about my circumstances – he'd attempt to help me. He told me of a friend of his who had a position in a company called the San Francisco chronicle. I'd heard of them although I've never read any material from the chronicle before. Well, they needed a new journalist.

He warned me that whilst I might not like it, it was better than nothing. Ross told me he'd get in touch with his friend and see what could be done.

Two days later I spoke with the friend, Richard. It was a long distance call that took several hours. We agreed to a starting date and an initial salary, along with a probationary period of six months based on my performance. Anything is better than my current job so I accepted and almost immediately telegrammed my Aunt Christy on the west coast, asking if I could stay with her for a while until I was settled.

Once my aunt confirmed this was alright, I tendered my resignation from my company, broke my lease with my landlord and started preparing the move. Now I am leaving tomorrow and could not be happier.

I'll give you my address in San Francisco below so we can keep in touch.

Cassandra

May 1938
San Francisco

Dear Sven,

Just a quick note to tell you that things are actually okay here.

Well, by okay, I mean I haven't killed anyone yet. The life in San Francisco is alien to me. I find it easy to get around but the charms of the west coast seem lost on me. I do not really want to be here but since getting a job back home is next to impossible and I'm really trying to lay low right now, I guess I do not have much choice.

I am living in the spare room of Aunt Christy's house. I cannot bloody stand that mutt of a dog that she keeps. The little bastard shits everywhere and for my aunt, this seems like a perfectly reasonable thing for it to do. She never house trained it – the other day I almost vomited over the stench in the living room.

My aunt and I do not really talk and I only seem to spend my time with colleagues from work. Mostly banal, middle aged men. I find this place to be dull and unfulfilled. It holds little interest to me. At least the job is alright, although I long to stand in a class room full of students, talking about the influence of Byron in the modern times instead of writing about the ills of the city.

Making my bed, I must lie in it now.

Nothing else to say. I do not feel any joy for being here.

Cassandra.

August 1938
San Francisco

Dear Sven,

So, its official eh? You're now working in the diplomatic department of Lisbon or something like that? Brilliant stuff – get as far south as you can from those fascist dogs as possible. Even if your new home is governed by Salazar – he has more sense than Hitler.

Still living with my aunt, although I'm actively looking for a place to rent now that I have a steady flow of money coming in. Being a journalist is not too hard – I can write and they like that bit. Spoke with Ross, the old friend of my dad's recently. He suspected I would not like being out here to begin with but he is urging me to be patient and just give things a chance. We'll see.

I shall be in touch. Nothing else to report. I hope the new job goes well darling.

Cassandra.

October 1938

San Francisco

Dear Sven,

Good day from San Francisco!

I decided to write to you again because I have good news. I am leaving my aunt's house to move into this two bedroom flat just below the Golden Gate Park. I am due to move in about two weeks and I could not be happier. My aunt is frankly annoying the hell out of me and it has been too long since I had my life back.

So, I'll be leaving at the end of October. My flat is currently uninhabited, although it might be that it is leased for an additional roommate soon enough. I do not mind the company as long as they're not a stuffy old prune like my aunt. I'll write to you again soon but I wanted to tell you that things are starting to look up for me.

The job at the chronicle is going well. I've been there for about half a year now. I'm not really in charge of anything specific right now; I am usually allowed to work on my own projects and I'm fine with that. So, for the most part I am satisfied with the stuff I am doing. Still considered a junior by many but far from it intellectually. Little else to report.

Sven, I really am glad that things in Portugal are working out for you. I should try and get work to assign me a trip to the country; we have working contacts over there which makes this a manageable idea. I really miss teaching and studying literature but I think I might be alright in San Francisco. At least now.

Cassandra

February 1939
Saigon

Dear Sven,

I wanted to start by apologising to you for not having kept in touch much since graduation. I still live in Saigon, working as a junior journalist for a firm that deals in the local politics. In many ways it is an incredible job, allowing me to live very well in Saigon without issues. I would probably look at being a senior journalist in the next five years – the progression in our Saigon office is very slow and people seem to live here for the lifestyle and not for the career goals.

But I shall be leaving Saigon in about three-four months to return to London. To keep you in the loop since contact has been awful lately; I came to Saigon in the summer of 1937. We finished university and I left to go home. I know you went back to Sweden and studied to become a member of the government or something along those lines. But since we last spoke, I extended my stay in Saigon through the firm and decided to remain out there for at least another year.

But now I will becoming home and wanted to tell you first. I have not even told my father yet. Maybe I can meet you in the next year or so and have a week of our old childish tricks?

I had really hoped that I would be better at this keeping in touch thing but it seems that too often something comes up and interrupts one from these essentials. But I wanted you to know that I frequently look back on our days at Princeton with joy, although I think we can both agree that in the last few months of my time there I was caught between the devil and the deep blue sea.

Things happened when we finished that led me to dread a life in London; so I applied for the Saigon office of a company that one of my lecturers knew. He put in a good word for me and without any delays I went to Saigon directly after University. My family hated the idea which only encouraged me to do it. My father and I were never that close anyway; he favours my two older siblings but I am unconcerned. He would not turn me away if I needed help because I am his blood and I have mostly been an offspring that was hassle free. But he also would not know what to do if I asked him for help that was outside his influence or wealth.

And as you will remember from our days in Princeton; my siblings do not like me and I do not care for them.

Sven, I'm sorry to trail off into another rant. I really hope you are well and that things are good. I hope that this letter reaches you. In truth, I do not know where you are living these days but I really hope that this letter finds you well. I have sent it to your family address in Stockholm; with a small slip requesting that it be sent to you if you are no longer there.

I would really like to meet back up with you in Europe at some point. I'll be back in London by roughly July at the latest. Until that time, I can be reached at our office in Saigon. I'll leave the address below; they know to forward me any missing mail if I leave and you respond after I go.

Yours,

Brian

February 1939
San Francisco

Dear Sven,

So today I spent the afternoon alone and miserable. Valentines Day has always been a shitty time of year and even as an academic, never mind a journalist, I have completely failed to understand the point of it. You can call it the position of a bitter cynic if you will but even when I courted men from my days of youth I never understood the logic of it. A day where couples remind each other that they do not actually despise their partners' faces but in fact are united by the grace of Eros while the rest of us are left to wallow in self-pity and starve ourselves because we're made to feel overly conscious of our actually attractive enough figures.

As I said - bunch of fucking nonsense.

I spent much of that Wednesday morning smoking cigarettes in the office whilst munching on biscuits. I was attempting to finish a piece on the personality of Howard Hughes - that billionaire playboy from Texas. I'd actually liked Hell's Angels when it was released although upon revisiting the film over Christmas I found that it was far from what I remembered ten years ago when it came out. Anyway, by coincidence our editor in chief asked me to conjure up a piece on Hughes for February.

I have about five days before the deadline - enough to throw some scrambled gibberish together. What mattered simply to be was not the craft of this piece nor the fact that I had been entrusted with the responsibility of representing the San Francisco Chronicle in this matter. No what mattered was that I'd be well paid for this project, all expenses covered. I have started to realise that the company having my name attached to it has led to certain benefits of which I am the primary benefactor. Namely job allowances and a decent salary, which are attached to the wider community of the city.

Yet for all that I still miss New York and my academic life. Sometimes I am an optimist but today even the optimists struggle to get it all right. It is strangely enough warm, well for the middle of February but I still felt the chill of the evening as I left the office around 5. I bought a bottle of red wine on the way home, smoked several cigarettes when I got back, finished the Hughes piece and was in bed by two. I decided to charge through the piece to avoid the crappy feelings that the 14th of February stimulates. I then quickly wrote this note for you. I'll send it off sometime this week.

Be well. Hoping that today was easier for you than I.

Regards,

Cassandra

May 1939
Saigon

Dear Sven,

How brilliant to hear from you! Too long my friend. I'm writing this letter to you in a rush but I wanted to send it off before works gets in the way again.

How are you? I think it is brilliant you are living in Lisbon. I have longed to visit there; I hear beautiful things about it. Do you plan to stay there long term or is this simply for a short while? You did not hint at the tenure of your stay there and I am most curious out it.

I'm leaving Saigon next month to come back to England – I'll send my replies to your address in Portugal unless told otherwise. Nervous about moving home is putting it mildly since I have completely forgotten how to live there.

Sincere apologies for how brief my letter is but I got interrupted on the last line and had to get a load of reports done by six pm. I'm finishing this up now and sending it before I forget.

Enjoy the weather in Lisbon. It never seems to get cold in Southern Indochina and I know it will be a shock being in England again.

Yours,

Brian

June 1939
Saigon

Dear Sven,

I have itchy feet again. I desire to travel again. I want to live in Europe again. I think coming home might work out for me. Living in England and being able to get to the mainland whenever I like. I can see this working out.

It is not like I have been given a choice anyway.

I look forward to being back in the old country. I have tired of this place.

I'll keep you posted.

Brian.

July 1939
San Francisco

Dear Sven,

Took a long walk in the city today as I contemplated my future here. I feel like things are better now than they have been – I at least get out of bed without the sheer loathing that I hold for myself. I mean, I put myself into this situation of being in San Francisco.

I felt stuck when I arrived because I felt shell shocked because having to leave Princeton and come here. I once held the position that few women could aspire to, never mind claim to have. That of a lecturer in a university that Europeans send their children to study in. a position of power that allowed me to showcase my knowledge and love for a subject.

And now I am here.

Here in this city on the other side of the country, trying to put my life back together. Whatever you want to call it. I definitely felt stuck in the beginning but I'm now at least adapting. I think moving out of my aunt's house helped. It was not right for a woman in her forties to have to spend time being dictated to by a stuck-up old crone. I at least have regained my sense of freedom.

Actually, in some ways being a journalist is not too bad. They pay reasonably well and I do not take shit from my colleagues. Every six months or so I seem to land some kind of promotion for my labour. The senior staff are impressed with my writing and the fluency in which I can process information and create pieces for the news-paper. This in itself is not something that I feel surprised by since I am used to churning essays out for people –

I've been doing it on a higher level since some of my colleagues were born.

One of my colleagues is this idiot called Susan, who I work with in the editing department. She is always acting like she is better than me since she worked there for several years. I turned up and quickly got to her paygrade and she thinks that because of this, she has the right to tell me how to work. The other day she criticised a piece I wrote for the Chronicle with another colleague – about the stylised and slick way we put the article together. I overheard her saying what a pompous arse I am in the staff room but did not say anything yet. I've learnt to keep my mouth closed and observe with my eyes for now.

I'm making another commitment right now. That is to absolutely not sleep with anyone in the office. Not only does it complicate things – it is also not what I need right now. True, I really enjoy sex but I'm trying to avoid it because of what happened with my fall from grace in Princeton. There is this one guy called Jeremy that I quite like but it is nothing beyond the desire to simply fuck him.

Sven, I must go. I'm due to head out this evening to a literature club that my friend Rosie is taking me too. I'm already late so I think I'll stop this letter now.

I wish you well in Portugal.

Cassandra

July 1939
London

Dear Sven,

I arrived home eight days ago from Saigon. A long and gruelling journey that took a nasty spell on me, I eventually stopped in Paris on route to rest, spending my time at one of my father's friends' homes until I'd rested sufficiently. All in all, I spent roughly two weeks readjusting to Europe. Paris is exactly how I recall it from my memories as a child.

I did consider calling in on you in Sweden but my reasons for returning home are because I have been reassigned to London and I have been here to discuss the contract with the recruitment in Paris. My father was pleased when we communicated that I was returning to Europe – his opinions on Indochina are unsavoury at best. I spent several days with family friends in Paris before returning to London after two years.

Reassigned; not a voluntary transfer. I was not entirely honest with you when we conversed in February. I had limited choice in what I could do about it but in some ways I believe leaving is the correct course of action. I feel as if I can accept it now and move on. So, I am now here, after being given three months of notice that I was to be reassigned. I did not want to go in the end, not really. If I continue with this company, I will be more successful in breaking into writing. Securing another job in Saigon is beyond difficult. And the lack of progression in the Saigon office compared to London is bonkers.

In the end, I did not complain about the opportunity to progress in London. But ultimately, this was not my decision.

The threat of war in Europe is indeed grave as I thought it was. It is difficult to keep track of events going on at home when you spend your mornings in an office and the afternoons in French-Vietnamese bars and do little else other than smoke opium. Indeed, I have come to realise that we ought to be very concerned and I do believe that a war in Europe is something we might have to be prepared for. The concept of two conflicts in twenty years seems bizarre to believe but it is starting to feel like these chaps mean business.

Anyway, I start work with the company on Monday. I'm staying at my brother's apartment until I get a place sorted out. He is barely home anyway, usually he is staying with this girl he is with or sleeping with, I'm not sure. I feel excited to start the work, although being here is alien to me. I spent the first eighteen or so years of my life here, moved to America for three and a half years, came home for a few weeks then left to go to Indochina. Two years passed and I do not feel attached to England. The thrill is gone from here.

Still, this might be until I find something better. Opportunities are limited in Indochina compared to Europe and I feel that I can progress to a higher position in a fraction of the time compared to two years as a junior journalist in Saigon. So I remain hopeful for the positive on this transfer. My hope is that I can readjust to living in London. It feels strange, cold and distant but I am hoping this is just an initial culture shock. It is good to be in the bubble of literature again. Some of our greatest writers walked these very streets and it feels incredible to know that this is the heart of literature.

By the way, have you read Hemingway's new novel, *To Have and Have Not?* It came out last year. A sterling effort and I highly recommend it to you. Are you still into Charles Dickens? Anyway, with all the books being brought out, it starts becoming impossible to keep up with who has written what but the nice thing about it is that we are not short of material to read.

Things in London are strange. Some old friends threw together a welcome home party for me at the Roxy about two days after I got back. I had not kept in touch with many in the almost six years of being gone from England but now I am keen to rekindle these friendships since I am an unknown in London. In my days of being a youngster, living in my family home and attending my studies, I'd frequent London on the weekends. But living in London is frankly not what I am used to, along with the dampness and the cold. Wearing a coat and scarf as opposed to a light shirt and chinos is not something I am adjusting to well.

I will see how things go for now. In many ways it is lovely to be back in an English speaking country and to see how the world really has not changed but I would be lying if I said I was not deeply troubled by the direction the states of Europe are moving towards. The shadow of fascism is indeed rising over the continent and I am deeply concerned that we are not handling these chaps in a sensible manner.

Then again, who really wants another war in Europe?

I'll be in touch and let you know how my time here goes. I wish you good health.

Yours,

Brian

August 1939

London

Dear Sven,

I see beautiful woman everywhere in London ; this encourages me to stick around. Take this one example the other week - a woman I saw whilst I was walking to the train station. A warm evening when the sun sets at 9.30 pm and everyone is forced to carry their blazer over their briefcase. I decided to relax and smoke in the sun before I took the train. I could easily smoke in the underground but I don't like the feeling of being suffocated.

As I stood inhaling my cigarette, I couldn't help but stare into the distance across the street at the nine to seven commuters charging to and fro. It was indeed that time of the day and I was quite alarmed by how the talks of war had permeated the streets of an otherwise uninspiring city. It is a curious horror to think that we could face conflict again with Germany after only just sorting the last mess out. I am not interested in war; nor do I want to be involved in conflicts with Germany but we might not be given any choice with the coming tide of military interventions in Europe.

Then I spotted her. Across from the street she walked in a beautiful red dress. The kind that suggested that she was going directly from work to a social affair, perhaps the opera. She held the class for such an occasion. I, on the other hand, was dressed in my second hand suit and tie. On this occasion I was without my hat (I woke later than my required time that morning and left my hat in the kitchen as I was rushing to catch the bus.) My tie was hanging loosely from my shirt collar with my top button undone, whilst my shirt itself was crumbled - all the fashion symptoms of a long day in a cluttered office.

As she stood next to me, reaching into her purse for what I could only presume where a packet of cigarettes, I could not help but feel profoundly self-conscious about the state of my image. The fringe of my hair was hanging forward in the summer heat and sweat had formulated on my brow.

I am sorry to drawl on about dull details of that evening. Anyway, before I could extinguish my cigarette, she turned and spoke softly, asking for a lighter having seemingly left hers someplace. So I obliged mine and watched as she inhaled the first puffs of nicotine, looking me in the eyes with her own green diamonds. Her hair was golden and long, her mouth the perfect small size I normally find on women of my own conquests. Her height slightly beneath mine, the red dress complimenting her figure brilliantly.

We made idle talk whilst I watched her smoke her cigarette, leaning against the red brick wall. Her smile, might flashed then for the first time, revealed pearls of white. She was beautiful.

London has been pleasant since I returned home because of moments like this. I live mostly alone in peace and through my solitude I can be rid of the arcadia of the city for roughly seven or eight hours of a day. Regents Park on the weekends and the trains to the coast just about keep the chances of a breakdown at bay.

Yours,

Brian

September 1939
London

Dear Sven,

We are at war. Europe is at war.

And so far, it seems we have little to fear. This could be open ended. Germany has lost before. We can win again. I have nothing to say beyond that. This has been a long time in the coming. The build up in the last year to this has been obvious.

And we are now here. So far, we have sworn to protect Poland, even though no action has been taken to halt the Axis powers and the Soviets have effectively divided the country up into bits. Poor sods have only just got their country back in the last twenty years before being torn up again.

And now it seems that we're in this shit with them. A dark winter awaits us.

I'm going to get drunk. I hate war.

Yours,

Brian

November 1939
London

Dear Sven,

We are at war indeed and yet all is quiet for now. I have just concluded lunch with my father at a club house in Guilford. His invitation, the car dropped me off at the train station back to London in time for an evening train. A very fancy joint – it was his invitation and he paid the bill.

I did not really want to go but he asked me because he wanted to know about my job. He did not ask about my personal life; he has assumptions and leaves it at that. I do not mind because he leaves me to my own devices and I to him. We have not exactly been close since my mother died and even then, he was an absent father. I suspect that he does this to curb his own guilt.

I do not dislike the old man. In a strange way, I love him. He has looked after me, helped me with my work and allowed me to exist outside of his world. He never asks me about my personal projects – but he did ask me to come to his firm and play my part in the family legacy. I told him that I'd see, that I want to follow my job in journalism for longer.

He does not approve but he is decent enough to leave me to my own devices. My brother, Clive, told him that I'm wasting my life but that I've always done this. How else do you explain the son of a wealthy lawyer who owns a firm in London who decides that he wants to be a writer? Well, I'm not a writer. I'm a reasonably experienced journalist who fantasies about being one.

Taking the train home, I continued to reflect on my father. About his life and his wishes. He has almost given up on me being anything of note, although he continues to protect me. We spoke of this coming war and he assured me that my job, along with his political influence, ought to keep the drafts and conscription at bay. I do not think I'll be involved in the front lines anytime soon.

This has relieved some of my anxiety. I had believed, with all sincerity that we would not be going to war with Germany. Chamberlain only assured the public last year in Munich that this was not going to happen. Nevertheless, here we are, about 12 months or so later. I would have stayed in Indochina if I'd have known this was going to happen. Despite the lousy pay and lack of progression.

I'm about to get off the train so I'll finish here. Hope you're keeping safe mate.

Brian.

December 1939
San Francisco

Dear Sven,

Just split coffee on my note book. Livid. Stained and damp from where it has gone everywhere. I'm hungover and struggling to make myself useful. We went out last night and went hard. Really hard. I've been kinda sleeping with someone over the last month but we broke it off a few days ago. Started developing feelings for each other and we both want to focus on our careers.

Bland eh?

I hope you have a lovely Christmas Sven. I'm staying at home this time, not doing much. Sarah, my roommate, and I are hosting a party later this week for our guests. She has actually been really good in encouraging me to meet her friends. Although I will tell you that this is mostly so we can have a good vibe in the house. Living with her is pretty easy – we do our own thing then occasionally meeting up on the weekends to have joint gatherings.

The issue of living here is that it gets so cold in the winter. If I could live in a warm country then I would. I cannot really leave the city because I need the work. I feel like my exile is slowly turning into a life I can enjoy. I dare not show my face in New York for a long time to come. I cannot face being there. I will stay here and face my life on my own terms, build a new realm here. I just want to be left alone a lot of the time. But I do not mind making new friends here. It does help.

But when they ask about how a woman with a strong east coast accent ended up here...well this is something I do not really want to discuss. With almost anyone. I probably converse with you about it over than anyone else.

Have a wonderful Christmas. Be safe in this war Europe is heading into.

Cassandra

January 1940
London

Dear Sven,

The foggy streets of London in winter – horror that needs no introduction. Oh and the cold. That icy chill that may as well permeate this entire country as if the borders of Scotland to Lands End. The absolute worst time of year and this winter has been horrendous. Trying to get up in the bitter mornings whilst not freezing to death is beyond difficult. It catches you by surprise and reminds us all that we cannot avoid the ice and snow.

Pessimistic you might think upon first reading this but I am missing the warm heat of Indochina, which is usually lovely at this time of year. I do not miss Saigon but at times like this I do long to return to a country where I won't die of hypothermia. But that is not going to happen now. We are locked in a stale mate with the Germans and until things start to change, we must all accept it for what it is. The political events of Europe are liable to kill any remaining flickers of joy for this country faster than my own attitude towards winter.

Lately I have felt depleted. I thought that I'd have a master plan in England that I'd be in the process of executing right now. But all I seem to do is get up, go to work and then attempt not to freeze to death in the evenings and early mornings. Witnessing the oriental man fishing on the mouth of the Tiền River and wandered shanty towns by the rivers in Indochina replay in my mind. Or the centre of Saigon, filled with heat and humidity that almost briefly banishes this cold...those things inspired me. The only inspiration right now is the reminder that England is at least welcoming to me.

Sorry to complain. You know I have always hated the winter time.

How are you doing? I can imagine that Lisbon is at least warmer than it is here. I am jealous since Portugal has always retained really good weather, even in the winter. Okay, well better than here.

I cannot really write anymore. It is eight in the evening and already so cold that my fingers are stiff. I have heated the flat but its limited owing to fuel consumption. Outside, in the communal garden is an air raid shelter that has been built. We have not used it yet and I hope never will. I walked into it the other day out of morbid curiosity – you know the things flood in winter? Here is hoping we can avoid this looming nightmare.

Thanks for listening to my rants Sven. I'm pissed off and frankly feel like I'm going to die in this winter. It is bloody rotten. At least the job is going well.

Brian.

March 1940
San Francisco

Sven,

Lots of scary news going on in Europe right now. The German army is on the march and the entire continent is in serious trouble. But you know this. Do not leave Portugal Sven. The Nazis will not attack the country because of Salazar – you will be safe there.

I thank God we are divided from these lunatics by two huge pools of water. I despise those dogs more than they hate us. But hate us they do and a fight is on our hands.

I sit in my office at work, smoking and jotting this note down to you. I think of you and I am concerned for you. For Brian too, although I imagine he seldom thinks of me these days. Going to meet some friends for a glass of wine later but hoping for you. We will raise a glass to our European friends tonight.

Don't die Sven. You are worth so much and I know that there are so many things you need to do.

Cassandra

April 1940
London

Dear Sven,

I walked through Hyde Park this morning, around 8 am before work started. It was one of those really warm mornings when the sun rises around 5 and I wanted to enjoy that feeling of witnessing the city waking up through without rushing through the bustling streets, dodging traffic on a second-hand bicycle. I felt peacefully calm given the fact that I was hurrying - work started at half 8 and I knew that going on foot would add an additional 30 minutes to my commute.

At this point I've been home for about a year. Tied over nicely with my job at the office, wooing various love-sick broads into my arms and spending my weekends in jazz cafes smoking cigarettes was what I consider a comfortable lifestyle for a late 20 something year old bachelor. But I constantly fret about my future, worrying about who I'll end up with, where I end up or what I'm so keen to do. I really want to write novels and live somewhere that matters. Somewhere which does not smack of nostalgic reference to imperialism.

The other night I stayed up with some friends till the early hours of the morning while we discussed what we wanted in our lives. I frequently harked back to my Princeton days during the conversation as if it was some point of when everything in my life radically changed. Since leaving America I've often floundered at the prospect of wondering if my life will ever hold consistency in monument towards something beyond making ends meet. I recall our days of when the hardest thing we'd have to deal with was kicking our previous nights conquests from our dorms and then struggling to emerge from our beds before noon. Ah, what life.

My friends seem to lack any desire to progress beyond the confines of London - I have lived in Indochina, earned a degree in politics and literature at Princeton, traveled America and screwed my share of Californians at the grand old age of 25. I feel somewhat superior to them with a touch of unintended arrogance. Maybe I've simply seen too much and not allowed them enough time to get through the unexpected brilliance of life. After all, I have been most fortunate in my time.

So after I left work (I refuse to talk about the 9-10 hours during work) I quickly sped home on the train, proceeded to change and shower before dashing back out 45 minutes later for drinks at a bar in the city centre. My company was mostly casual pals along with one or two friends from a literature class that I have been taking on the side (my engagement on Monday and Thursday evenings at Goldsmiths College.) The night was boozy and smoky. Absolute organised chaos as Robin attempted to mobilise the hoard, of which I was a member, through the streets of Camden. Never made it home, woke up with the world's worst headache and two strangers on each side of me - one was clearly female, the other male.

Great, so I managed to end up in a threesome and was incapable of summoning any memories of how this had happened aside from the girl tugging on my arm at the pub and the man winking at us. I knew the guy - Dennis from the literature class, was not invited, turned up anyway as a straggler. Creep. No idea about the girl. Probably Dennis' sister. The man was that abstract and frankly weird. Wonderful situation...

Thank heaven it was a Saturday that morning so I could limp home and die in my bed. Saturday merged seamlessly into Sunday whilst I struggled to not perish in the haze. The pain was so ghastly I never wrote more than two words of writing that day - incidentally it was 'bugger off.' Recollecting anything beyond that of my Saturday is a bonus. Sunday was forgettable. Fell asleep around 10 pm. Woke up late (again) on Monday morning mistakenly believing that it was still the weekend.

I feel a bit grossed out by the last 72 hours to say the least but since you asked how I was getting on...

Yours,

Brian

August 1940
San Francisco

Dear Sven,

I'm trying to write to you whilst hungover and hungry. Today is a Monday morning. I'm resigned to a headache that'll probably last half a week. I spent Friday hosting guests with my flatmate Sarah. Saturday was a long lunch that turned into an expensive session of booze. Sunday was whiskey in the house whilst I worked on this weeks project.

I often wonder if I'm an alcoholic. I drink because it makes getting through the day easier than without. I do not turn down a drink if one is offered although I can go without if I must. But I prefer not to. The cigarette smoking is still there; I don't think I'll get off the shit soon. But I have not given up my hard work ethic or my passion of living how I want. These are my only vices, although exercise wouldn't be a lousy decision.

The job is going well. The apartment I rent is stunning. The recent construction of the Golden Gate Bridge can be seen from our balcony. The city is not New York. It is different. Hills dominate the scenery and in the distance you can see the island of Alcatraz. A mix of the rough with the beautiful – San Francisco may yet prove to be a diamond in the rough.

I look at myself in the mirror, writing naked as I sometimes do when I'm alone. I feel healthy and well and for 45 I am not unattractive. My breasts, although starting to age with time now, are still perky enough. My thighs are reasonably toned as I walk everywhere over this hilly city. My hair, now shorter and slightly greying, is still thick and blonde, the way you might remember it. Age is dawning on me in these days but I still feel youthful enough to act accordingly; wiser though but not a great deal more it seems.

Age is an interesting idea. I feel that many women at this age, start to have a crisis of life. They feel that the best years are behind them. For me, the best might yet be to come. I work for myself and live for myself. I do not regret avoiding family life, but I wonder if this feeling will change when I am an old woman. To be continued I imagine. You'll forgive my slurry way of explaining things; I do not know why I have chosen to discuss these subjects. I am tired and frankly I think I need sleep. Or sex. Then sleep. Maybe both.

I would like to take a return trip to Europe. I have not been since the twenties when I was in Berlin. I cannot imagine how that city has changed now. Too different, too fascist. I knew a student in Princeton who had a overtly fascist father who had an empathetic streak for Hitler's policies on Jews. He sounded or sounds, I do not know if he still lives, like a disgusting man. But fascism has and always will be a disgusting ideology. I fear that Spain is due to have a rough couple of years with that prick Franco ruling the roost.

I have to go to bed. I am exhausted and writing this has finished me off. My hangover is slow burning and has only worsened with the passing of the evening. I cannot continue anymore.

Cassandra

Part II

August 1940
London

Dear Sven,

We've watched the RAF and the Luftwaffe tear up the skies of England over the last month. The Battle of Britain, as Churchill named it, has been in full swing. And to my surprise – we're winning. At no small cost, but winning nevertheless.

We've feared invasion almost directly after the last of our forces fled the beaches of Dunkirk. And yet, so far the fighting has mostly been restricted to the might of the German air force and their considerably smaller but dedicated opponents of the RAF. I, like many others, know that it is the grace and courage of our men, with little else but small planes and comradeship that has kept these devils at bay.

The other night I sat on a roof top terrace that was open to the public, drinking a beer and smoking cigarettes with several colleagues and this attractive girl I was attempting to bed. Across the sky and through the clouds of a thunderstorm, we could make out the sounds of engines. The engines of what the bartender told us was a Focke-Wolf 190 and a Hawker Hurricane in a dodge fight. What I briefly mistook as flash of sheet lighting became obvious as an explosion as one of our boys blew a Jerry out of the sky.

A cheer when up from the bar, like we were watching some game of football where the team you hated was loosing on their own turf. Despite this, I found myself reflecting philosophically on the bus home before dark – this man we cheered as he burnt to death in his plane had a family. Probably a mother or father, at least a girlfriend back in some small village in Bavaria or something. And we all cheered anyway as he roasted alive in that plane. Do not get me wrong; rather him than one of our own. It did not stop me feeling lousy about it.

We've had the Battle of Britain turn some sort of tide for the immediate future. Germany knows after this that we as British are made of stern stuff and unwilling to give up easy. We've made it clear to the Axis powers that we do not consider surrender an option; yet how long will we last? I can only hope that some day this war will end, with us coming out in a position where we can all look back and breathe relief. Those days are far from us right now. All we can do is survive each day and hope.

I envy your safety right now. It is not safe for us to be out on the streets or after dark. Despite the protection my job offers, I cannot help but fear being called up to serve for my country. I'm no coward but I do not want to die.

But know that in this moment, writing this letter, I am alive and well. The night did not end too badly. Brought that girl home with me. Won't be seeing her again – too clingy and wanted to know if I'd like to settle down in light of this crazy war. Not a bad bit of stuff though.

Take care Sven. I'm trying to do the same – B

October 1940.
San Francisco

Dear Sven,

I regret to start writing to you after a spell of being quiet to tell you that Aunt Christy died yesterday afternoon. I was at work when I was contacted. As her next of kin and only relative living in California I was the logical choice for the doctors. I was aware that she was unwell; however, it seems she was rushed to hospital about two days ago after being falling down some steps. Since yesterday was a Friday, I was able to go to the hospital after lunch and was told to take the rest of the day off once I explained the circumstances to my colleagues.

Her passing was peaceful – she was completely unconscious by the time I arrived. I am conflicted. On one hand she was a terribly depressed woman who had lost her husband in the Great War; she never remarried nor indeed did I think she ever have anyone after my uncle was killed. She disapproved of my hedonistic lifestyle and felt I was going against the grain because of a damaged childhood.

Yet, she had warm moments. After all, she took me in when I came to San Francisco and even helped me find the apartment I live in. She read my articles in the Chronicle, not because she agreed with what we write but because it was out of respect to me. Occasionally, when she was in good moods, she could be great.

And it dawns upon me that she was the last living relative I openly talked to. My own life has had its ups and downs but I did always have a soft spot for the old bag. Needless to say, I will miss her in a strange way. Seems she died without leaving a will – I do not believe her death was anything beyond premature. She was several years my uncle's junior and only a dozen or so years older than me.

It would be a fair comment from me to tell you that I will not be writing again for a while. There is the funeral to sort out, the issue of what becomes of her house and the rest. On a somewhat positive note, I am pleased to tell you that her mutt will not be an issue; it was run down by a fire truck in the late summer.

Yours,

Cassandra

November 1940
London

Dear Sven,

We are well and truly under attack. The most recent Blitz bombing was two days ago on Coventry. Our office covered the news on behalf of the local area in Chelsea and Kensington; it is not pretty. The city is in ruins and without power – in the winter of all times. Still, the relief effort to help citizens is absolutely incredible and the coming together of all peoples to help each other is inspiring.

There have been cases of anti-Semitism at work though. One of my colleagues, this idiot called Hamilton (already sounds like a toff right?), thinks that Jews cannot be trusted and that they would be the first to raid the ruins of houses and steal property. The man is an idiot and regretfully my superior in the office. I do my best to avoid him at all costs but I caught him talking like a fascist lately about how we need to all be watchful of this threat in London.

I've got nothing against Jews, Negros or the rest. I cannot say I really know many but after spending so much time in Indochina; my mind is not closed. They're just people and only trying to survive through this horror like the rest of us. Indeed, it is actually contrary to our stand against fascism to adopt these principles. I felt like saying to that tosser Hamilton the other day that if this was his attitude, maybe he should join the Nazis that just destroyed Coventry.

Walking through London, the damage is crazy. My flat has been spared any harm, although two streets down was hit by a bomb not that long ago. It sent everyone into a panic. It was brief though and instead of causing "an every man for himself" attitude, we pulled together to make sure the elderly and the children got out first. Sitting in an air raid shelter with about a dozen or so other residents, we told jokes, play charades and read to each other stories of a comedic fashion to pass the time.

When the all clear finally came, we emerged and simply got on with our lives again. I have to admit that despite the carnage the Jerries are causing; we're unusually calm about it and the bombs are something of a daily routine rather than a fear factor that causes us all to live in despair and doom. The Prime minister is due to make a speech in the House of Commons and on the radio later today. I do not get tired of hearing the old man's voice – Churchill is a beacon of hope right now, despite everything else.

Not all of it is fun and games though. Walking through a badly bombed part of London the other week, I saw a small child on the ground, dead. She had been killed by an explosion that turned her skin into burnt flesh...her mother wailing on the floor, clutching onto what remained...I felt sick to my stomach and had to keep moving. I did not leave her alone as she had two members of the fire service and a warden with her. Instead I went to the nearby stand, serving tea and offered my services. I dared not look back at the mother and her grief.

God damn the black souls of these murdering bastards.

You do not need to worry about me. Know that I am jealous of your situation in Portugal with the warmer weather and immediate safety that your country is in. Hitler will not attack you. The politics of your country should keep you well and truly out of this war.

On the lighter note of my love life. Ha! What love life? I've been picking up girls from time to time and engaging in some seedy behaviour. It passes the time and helps me relax after stressful days in the office and the genuine fear that each day might be my last. I do not believe in love or any of that. Had all of that damaged beyond repair after the last time I attempted to love someone. No one I pick up is worth keeping. I just sleep with them for my pleasure. They're alright but nothing compared to what I would prefer in life – but this seems incidental compared to my past and immediate future, given how gloomy everything feels right now.

So we're all still here and hopefully will still be here by the time I next write to you. England is holding, despite the brutality of these lunatics of the Third Reich. Let us hope that they run out of fuel and drop into the English Channel!

My best wishes to you Sven.

Brian.

December 1940
San Francisco

Dear Sven,

Happy holidays! I have never really cared for Christmas, preferring to spend it in Cape Cod instead of New York. This marks my second December in California and my first without Aunt Christy.

Allowing you to experience my feelings as close as possible over dried ink several weeks after receiving and reading it, you will no doubt detect a sense of sadness for me. The truth is that I feel indifferent. I never really knew the woman; she was the sister of my father and I'd only met her a handful of times. We rarely had dinner together after the first month and by the time I had come to move into my apartment, I had not really seen her for several weeks.

There were some innocent explanations. A difference of lifestyle; I had the job for the Chronicle before I left the east coast, she and the mutt frequently attended social gatherings and occasionally I went home with others. Then there are more sinister explanations; she was a devout catholic whilst I was not, she preferred the company of old women and fine gardens as I spent my days reading in our backyard or at work – you might say we did not really include each other.

Did I really like her? Not really. We split the bills for her house and she saw me as a cash converter even though her brother-in-law is a wealthy man who refuses to acknowledge me. She failed to understand my love of literature or my desire to work in something that I considered meaningful (journalism is far from meaningful when one compares it to the pursuit of literature but it beats sitting at home and wasting my time.) She banned smoking indoors, forbade the discussion of religion since my opinions offended her and sincerely loathed the idea of sex out of the marital bed.

I do not miss her. But I felt sorry for her. She frequently spoke of her late husband and how he had died in the name of God against the heretics (even though those people of Germany shared her core beliefs.) That he had been taken from her too soon but she was bound by the honour of his death and her faith in God to remain married to him even in death and thus celebrate; until God had 'reunited them in heaven.'

If I must speak openly of her and how I feel then it is that I pitied her but by the time we came to know each other she was already too far in the rabbit hole to be saved. She was indeed my family and I mourn her accordingly, though I do not consider it a personal loss to my overall life that she is now reunited in heaven with her husband. May her repressive sexual nature be dealt with in whatever way the ghost of her husband sees fit. But although it is no personal loss to me, I am sorry she is dead.

I am spending the winter in Hawaii with this model that I am sleeping with. He earns loads of money and prefers older women. Naturally, I talked him into the trip as I wanted to just get away from it all. I believe he wants something more serious as he is looking at changing his career as he fears his looks will fade prematurely and thinks my income might be the answer. I do not want a partner. I want lovers, but I do not want to be committed to anyone right now. I enjoy my own company when I do not require affection and I prefer that mentality.

I wish you a wonderful holiday in neutral Portugal and please let me know what you are doing for Christmas. I am excited – I have never been to Hawaii.
With love from Cassandra

January 1941
London

Dear Sven,

You need to tell me positive things on your end. I want to know more about this girl you've started dating in the last few months. Who is she? What does she do? Does she have a good body and give you sexual satisfaction? You must like her if you are inviting her to move in with you. I cannot believe you are already talking of settling down with her but it is clear that you are in love. I am happy for you Sven. Truly, you deserve to be loved because you are the most wonderful man I know.

I went home with someone yesterday night. A good session in the sheets made sure that I could forget the stress and nightmares of the Blitz lately. People of my circle are drinking like the world is coming to an end and getting into bed with each other is a good way of admitting that our stiff moral values are futile when we are under constant attack. I don't know if I'll see her again, but after this incident of near death, maybe I might.

You see, I woke up on this Sunday morning to another air raid siren. The sound drowned out my very mind as I fell from the girl's bed, struggling to get my trousers on, both of us rushing for the door and into the communal garden where the rest of the house was already crowding into the shelter. Realising that I had left my shirt inside and that I had a mere stitch of clothing covering my waist it was clear that I'd simply have to get on with this and hope to hell a bomb didn't hit the flat. Or the shelter.

After about 45 minutes, the chaos settled and some form of civility returned to the region, so I decided to get out and return home. Kissing the girl goodbye and giving her my office address in case we needed a second fuck later, (something about nearly being killed in an attack does this to you) I took off on my bicycle and went into the city centre. Arriving about an hour later by St Paul's, I observed the damage caused by the bombers. Small fires and rubble that weren't there last time but now littered some streets. Beyond that very little at all. Another lousy day in January from what we had experienced thus so far.

As I'm writing this now, I cannot help but feel a sense of dread that we've been dealing with this since last September. But I am trying to be positive so expect my details of these situations to be summary at best. Morale in London is good enough when you consider the context of the situation. Neighbours stay in each other's pocket's whilst the bombs continue to drop. Death does not necessarily hang over the city but storm clouds are occasionally on the eastern skies.

I recently read that the damage in London is incredibly minor compared to the far east of Europe. We cannot possibly know what ever happened in Poland after we left the mainland but one thing is for certain – God help us all from this war machine. I am frequently finding myself thinking about the horrors going on in France. I wonder how it will be should I ever go back. If I even want to after this war ends, should this war end...or if I'm even still alive by the end of it...

I wish to be positive but I remember the first day of the bombings in September. It was a bright, sunny day and I was in Hyde Park with some friends. We had bottles of wine and cigarettes, with good company and enjoyable weather. We knew that things were sour in mainland Europe; yet with the success of the Battle of Britain, I felt that we would enjoy something of a pleasant period of calm. And I remember the first time I heard the sirens and we felt a collective sense of dread lingering in the air. London was on fire as the sun went down that evening.

Time stood still at that hour. The sky, once clear and beautiful, turned dark by the hornets which swarmed the horizon. The noise drowned out the laughs and delights of the day. Then the bombs dropped and the city turned to chaos in front of our eyes. Panic gripped those who were only minutes ago calm and optimistic...No I have to stop. I cannot put this into words for you. I have simply never seen anything so frightening in my life and I hope I never will again.

I'll never forget that day for as long as I live.

Brian.

February 1941
San Francisco

Sven,

I broke it off with the model I was dating. Turns out he was an asshole because he was sleeping with someone else whilst telling me it was not just sex. So I've finished with him. I will not be treated as some second rate skank. I mean, I do not mind having one night stands with men and I've definitely slept with friends. But when someone treats you like you are exclusive by taking you to Hawaii then fucks other women behind your back – I mean seriously?!

So I dumped him and went on a two day bender over the weekend and stayed at a friend's apartment. We ended up having sex several times. Nothing serious, we both just needed to blow off some steam. I hadn't slept with him before but it was fun. I think we'll both just keep it as friends but it helped get my mind off the model.

A week or so past and I was over him. Otherwise the last few months have been quiet. I've managed to get through a lot of negativity and sort my life out. I am pretty stable in the apartment and getting on with life. Sarah provides a lot of laughs and my colleagues are proving to be pretty encouraging of my abilities.

I've become pretty successful at work. I have a lot of praise for my work and I get by well. I have a high rapport with people. I will put myself back on the scene soon, once I get things together. For now I'm quite happy to keep going and just see what happens with life. Americans are not too concerned by war, even though we seem to be happily approaching a conflict with the Axis powers. We cannot go on supplying the Allies without some type of consequence.

Hope you're alright Sven. Give my love to your wife.

Cassandra

May 1941
San Francisco

Dear Sven,

I've had a fight with a friend today. She called me a fucking bitch when I disagreed with her openly on the subject of the Nazis. It hurt and frankly I do not think we will recover from it. No one calls me a fucking bitch! She is no one special to me. Not really – few people are.

I limped home and decided to write to you about it whilst drinking coffee and reflecting in the warm light of the afternoon sun. The sun that always makes things feel better. I've got a review on a book that I need to hand in for tomorrow so I'll be keeping this to a brief piece of news. So far in my job, so good. Living in the city? Well, I suppose it is okay but I find that it still lacks the buzzy nature of New York.

I miss New York sometimes. When I came out here it was for work and I did not enjoy the hills, the food or even the vibes the city offers. These days I have acclimatised but not without having to forget what New York is like. It feels increasingly like it is a distant memory. San Francisco has slowly become my home and one I am getting used to.

But my 'friend' insulting me makes me nostalgic for my home. My first home. I think this is why I decided to write to you. Because I miss the earlier times.

Tensions have started mounting with Japan lately over the issues of fossil fuels that America has been supplying to the country. I fear that we will end up becoming involved in a conflict with them in no time at all. This concerns me since none of us want another war. I've already lived through one and can readily recall the horrors of it. Funny how the bad you can recall quite easily but the good, like New York...well that just becomes more of a distant memory in time.

No amount of wishing will recover the times we had so I will leave it there. All I can say is that we wake up, trying to be optimists and fall hard on our faces.

Otherwise I am alright.

Yours,

Cassandra

June 1941
London

Dear Sven,

Today was a delightful Sunday afternoon.

Experiencing a rare weekend day without a crippling hangover to trial me until the early hours of Monday morning, I found time to go running in the morning then successfully made it to Roger's for around midday without incident. Roger is a 30 something-year-old stock broker who lives in middle class Chelsea with his Danish wife, Hannah. Reminds me of one of your sisters actually. Beyond her immediate beauty I could recall no consistent details of her – I met her briefly two years ago. Quite a mystery that I cannot recall more. An even bigger mystery is how she ended up with Roger.

Whilst eating lunch with six or seven other guests, I struggled to come to terms with the idea that this too could one day be my future. Everyone I saw in that room seemed happy, content, incurious, mildly fulfilled and with a touch of irony perhaps, uninterested in my tales from America or Indochina. We had absolutely nothing in common; save the fact that we all knew Roger and his darling wife in one respect or another.

Desperately requiring a cigarette, I was offered one by Hannah as we both walked to the garden (Roger didn't allow smoking in the house, despite the addiction that plagued the majority of the guests.) Sitting on the garden bench as the afternoon progressed towards four pm, Hannah took the time to tell me that I was a good sort of bloke, albeit young and brash but not the cynical man I feared I was heading towards. She said that she could understand how I sometimes felt as a person who really did not belong in England.

My only real connection to the country is by that of birth and national identity. Beyond that, I do not hold much attraction to this place, nor do I understand what I am doing here. As a Dane, she told me that her own appeal to England had been simply because her country was presently occupied by the Germans and that she simply could not go home. Denmark might have not suffered the same extent of violence and mayhem that other countries endured but the rule is simple - she cannot leave this island. Even this letter, sent to you in Portugal will probably be read and then reread by the authorities before it even makes it to your front door.

So, we sat and smoke our cigarettes whilst discussing surprisingly mature topics (all the others wanted to discuss how they loved their 9-5 office jobs and their mutual disgust of Germans). As it was the two of us were the ones who'd been to Berlin, Hannah having visited the capital several times given the geographical relationship between Denmark and Germany - she was native to the city of Tønder.

I went to Berlin one summer with my family as a small boy. Our mutual understanding that Germany was not all the black and white who-ha that our contemporaries sketched it out to be made reconsider my position, allowing me to be very grateful that she was there. I adore Scandinavians anyway as you know, but her personality was a cheery bonus. We agreed on another side to the people of Germany, those who were normal, sane...human. Fundamentally we were both a bit disgusted by the casual racism that permeated the dining hall. Words that held no pleasantries and were riddled with ignorance.

I felt sorry for her own difficulties, given that her country had been occupied by the German forces even though we had agreed that they weren't all monsters beyond redemption or reason.

This reassured me that at least some of the company I keep in England is not blinded by the ignorance of racism. I always looked back to our cosmopolitan gang in America and how such bigotry was simply absent from our company. True, we debated, discussed and fought the subject at every turn within the confines of our university halls but we never faced this casual stupidity from people who we'd think were rational and educated. Education does not always rid an individual of his naivety. Nor does it safe guard one from falling back into this abyss of ignorance.

I went home that evening feeling that I had made a friend in Hannah. Not just a friend but an ally that was like minded and intelligence. Something of a nomad, a person without a clear-cut allegiance to a nation, donning different layers of identity. Obviously a cultured and educated woman in her own right - an absolute rarity in this day and age. How on earth a man of Roger's standing ended up with her is beyond me. I nodded off to sleep around about two, shortly after composing this letter among other things. I slept soundly and even though I was up again within four and a half hours time the pleasant mood of that Sunday afternoon resonated throughout the following day. I was happy.

Yours,

Brian

October 1941
San Francisco

Dear Sven,

I've decided to visit New York in December for Christmas. I was actually invited by a friend called Jordan, who I used to teach with in my earlier days. He is now a professor of the University of New York and an old buddy from days far gone.

I must confess – I am surprised he has reached out to me. We have hardly spoken these past five years. In his letter, he said that was entirely his point and that five years should not turn into ten. So, I am going to leave for New York on December 22nd and I will return to the west coast around the 2nd or 3rd of January. Our office is closed until the 5th so I have enough time to readjust from this time away.

In many ways, I need it. Although I have been promoted at work several times since I started and, established a reputation as one of the best journalists in the company – it comes with a price. I'm working unusually long hours right now and fighting tooth and nail to get the best leads in the company. Many seem to underestimate me, purely because I am a woman. The surprise of this is that it actually gives me an edge. I can think like a man and my rivals in the office have not come to realise this until recently.

I'm actually very excited for the break. It is something to look forward to and beats last year of feeling regretful over Aunt Christy. I'm over her death, well and truly by now. It did not make it any easier though in context – she was still family. Reconnecting with some of my old friends might give me a sense that I am still liked. This job of mine makes you either of two things – respected and feared or bullied and abused. I am the former of the two but the worst thing remains. I am unloved.

So maybe this might give me the opportunity to reclaim some of those old times and allow me to be positive about my life. True, I have friends (and lovers) in the city but few I would say I am close to. Even my housemate Sarah, who I frequently share laughs and happy moments with, is not close to me. They do not know me that well, if at all. I could use something like that to give me momentum in life.

And in the background of all this misery and complaining, people continue to get on with their lives.

How will you spend Christmas Sven? Would you be able to get it off from work, even though everyone is flat out with the conflicts in Europe right now? And are you happy in your life still? I often wonder about you and how you managed to be the best of us all.

Yours,

Cassandra

October 1941
London

Dearest Sven,

A thousand apologies for the radio silence lately. I'm still alive and breathing.

You old dog! I am proud of you mate – getting that girl to fall in love with you so. She sounds like a wonderful person and the photo that you sent me with this letter now sits on my desk in the office. I smile whenever I look at the two of you on the beach. Though I'd never thought I'd say it, the life of a civil servant suits you my friend.

I recently bumped into someone I knew in a café. Roger's wife, Hannah. I was drinking a coffee, smoking like a chimney and scribbling in my notebook about ideas for a story. I'm still trying to come up with ideas for a book. Narrowly avoiding death numerous times in the last year makes you realise that you need to action your ideas and one thing I crave more than anything is to be a successful writer. So, I've been trying very hard to write a story.

But I suffer from a block. I cannot seem to formulate a story that holds water. I do blame the past for this. Literature was always something I found hard to break into – like so many unpublished writers. I do not believe I stand a chance. It makes me despair and it was on that Saturday afternoon, hungover and tired that I attempted to write my own stuff for the first time in a long time.

And it was proving to be impossible. I struggle to get the words out. It does not help that all of my creative energy is clogged because of the workload we have in the office. I ordered another coffee, lit another cigarette and stared at the pittance that I had come up with so far. I'm not a serious writer, this much is obvious. I often day-dream of writing a book, occasionally spend a solid hour working, and then get distracted by other things. Not just the environment of England right now; I simply cannot focus.

As I sat in silence staring at the semi-blank pages, a woman's gentle voice bid me good afternoon. I turned and found myself staring into the beautiful Danish eyes of Hannah, who directly took a seat opposite me and smiled, cheerfully ordering a café latte as she did so. The café was rammed and I had retained my seat for several hours – she told me she'd just arrived and wanted to say hi.

I had not seen Hannah since that lovely afternoon in the summer at Roger's place. Indeed, I was a bit surprised that she recognised me but I quickly fell into a conversation that was delightful and easily engaging. She had not realised at first that I was attempting to work and apologised; blushing, I told her to stay. We quickly came to the subject of my supposed ambitions. This is something I am reluctant to tell people about since I am profoundly self-conscious as a writer. It was also something that vanished entirely when I found myself talking to her.

Indeed, although we had only met twice before and this was indeed a chance meeting, the conversation was natural. Easy, engaging and full of laughter. She is without a doubt a person of incredible interest and I am openly envious of Roger and how he lucked out with such a fascinating person. By the time it came to pay the bill and leave, it was almost closing time. But the conversation never dragged and we found that there was a lot of mutual interest. We discussed books, talked of travel, our love of bicycles and our dislike of the political right at home and abroad.

Although she is married, she rarely spoke of Roger. Instead she gave me her full attention during our chance encounter and encouraged me to speak of my book. Or lack of it but she had a genuine interest. And unlike others, such as Cassandra, who viewed me as holding a flight of fantasy or my father, who views novelists as lazy; she seriously believed that what I was talking about was not the idle thoughts of some young man. Instead she urged me to take my ideas seriously and told me that I either need to stop doing it or jut do it and not care about those past opinions.

I paid the bill and decided that this need not be a chance encounter. I gave her my address in London and suggested a meeting in the future. To my astonishment, she said yes directly. I felt that her being married and hanging out with a single man of my standing would be an immediate no; yet she almost seemed humbled and happy that I asked her.

I walked her to the bus. She seemed unconcerned about spending all afternoon with me when she probably had a prior engagement. Her parting words to me were to not feel that I had dominated her time; my time with her was the gift. We spoke of meeting up sometime in the next couple of weeks, social lives permitting and having another long talk like the one today.

Sven, do not get ideas. She is lovely and radiant, offering so much in a time of gloom. But she is married to Roger. The idea of pursuing anything beyond friendship seems a flight of fantasy to me. I'd be lucky to maintain anything beyond the memories of this magical afternoon with her.

I wish you all the love and luck in the world with your new girl my friend.

Brian.

December 1941
San Francisco

Dear Sven,

So, war has finally happened. We are at war with Japan.

Our country has taken a battering like no other. The horrors created on Hawaii with those poor bastards that burnt in the sea has devastated us. A surprise attack – we never saw it coming.

I went to Hawaii about a year ago with that model, Max. A stunning island that will be changed forever. The world is at war again. Japan has decided with war against nation was inevitable and have obviously struck first. So, whatever comes from this, who knows? We are involved in the destruction of Germany and Japan now.

The USA is strong and we will hold the line against these aggressors. The unprovoked attack will be their undoing. We stand with the world against them. I fear the worst now – it seems you are in the only neutral country now. The whole world is at war it seems apart from your home. I do not know what will happen. No one does. But I think the USA will tip the balance against the Axis powers.

I'm going to leave for New York in a few weeks time. Work is swamped right now but I think it'll calm down and not interfere with my trip to the east coast. I'll be able to take the time off – going to need it after the next few weeks.

Be safe Sven - we are all in danger these days.

Cassandra

December 1941
London

Dear Sven,

A glimmer of hope on the horizon that never felt like it was coming!

America has entered the war...I cannot believe our good fortune. We stood on the brink of invasion and death. Hitler invades the USSR – score one for taking the focus off our island, although we still struggled on. Then, after the massacre at Pearl Harbour, he makes the insane decision to declare war on the USA. Despite the horror of those poor yanks that were roasted alive in a cowardly surprise attack, there was open celebration in our office when news first came in.

It was the first time I'd seen everyone so happy. Even that wanker Hamilton and I raised a glass together in a moment of sheer joy. We might have a chance after all. The streets of London feel like they have vibrancy to them that I have not seen since the summer of 1939.

This letter must be brief since I am due to go to work in half an hour but I wanted to give you a quick update on things.

Still barely any work done on my book since you last asked me. I have some ideas that might be worth mentioning, once I get them processed but it remains some blind-sided idea that might happen one day. I do want to do it but I simply do not think I am good enough. I am not Conrad, Hemingway or Austin. Some a college boy who writes articles for a magazine company in London. I am told what to write; I am not paid to come up with my own work and my ideas remain unfulfilled.

I saw Hannah for the third time recently. We met at a bar in central London after I finished work. It was the first time we had drunk alcohol together and she was surprisingly open about herself. Instead of keeping the conversation on me and my work, she talked to me in a manner I had not suspected. About her unhappiness at home and how she and Roger had drifted apart. That when they started, he was charming and sweet but six years of marriage had left him a stranger in the house.

Okay, I'm sexually attracted to her. You correctly guessed this the last time we spoke of her. But I really behaved myself around her. I held her gaze, talked to her as my equal, not as I do with one of my usual conquests. I offered her opinions about life and told her my own stories of being alone and how I observed people. We laughed a lot and at one point, she briefly touched my arm and shoulder, almost by accident, yet retained her hold for a second longer as we looked each other in the eyes.

The temptation to kiss her was there; direct and evident. Yet I smiled and retained my gentlemanly composure; she is a petal flower, dancing in the wind that provides a source of joy in this gloomy and damaged land. I concentrated so hard on the conversation that I even ignored a patron in the bar whom I knew from a previous drinking session or two because I was so keen to talk to her.

She has invited me to come to a social affair next weekend as her guest. When I asked if Roger would be jealous, her reply was that she'd doubt he'd notice. I immediately pretended I did not have any plans that weekend and told her I'd be thrilled to come with her to this occasion. It is the first time she has asked me to something like this and I'm really interested in her.

I am fearful though. Fear of being hurt, the fear of this being another Cassandra. The fear of being viewed as boring. Between us chaps, the fear of being type-cast as homosexual because I have not made a move on her. I have refrained from this because she is married and I am being respectful but also because, to me, she is not just anyone.

Fear does stupid things to us but I do not want to do something stupid out of fear and risk ruining what is becoming a meaningful friendship. Maybe your advice is correct; that I should just stay my course. Sleeping with married women or those who have important attachments is never a sensible idea. I learnt that from Princeton.

But I really want her. Help me Sven. I have started to develop feelings for her.

Yours my friend,

Brian.

January 1942
New York

Dear Sven,

I am in New York right now, having come here for Christmas. I'm regretting it now. I feel like this place has changed and is far from the buzzy city I can recall. Or maybe I've changed and no longer feel like I used to live here. It remains unclear. The issue with New York seems to be me. I just think I should have stayed in San Francisco.

You never realise just how big the states are until you move around and see it for what it is. The west coast is different somehow and does not have such a high tolerance for people being liberal. True, it is a liberal city in how it treats blacks, Hispanics and Jews. It is pretty alright with that and the lingering stench of Jim Crow that has haunted the south for so long is not to be found here.

I grew up in Maine as you know and moved to New York before I came to Princeton. Most Americans that I have met seem to stay in the same city for considerably longer than I do; moved about a fair bit before I settled on the west coast. I feel like it is my home now and New York is becoming a distant memory.

You might be asking then why I came back to New York for Christmas and New Year's? The answer is twofold; San Francisco has been a bit difficult lately with the outbreak of war and I needed a good break from it. The second reason is that I was invited by my friend Jordan; who used to teach at Princeton and the party host. Jordan has a pretty big apartment in the city with enough room to host numerous guests. It was basically ten days of drinking too much.

But things with a mutual friend who was at the party made it difficult. The reception was cold like the weather. He seemed a bit off with me. No idea what he'd been saying or thinking – everyone else was alright with me. I never understood why men behave so strangely with women after sleeping with them. We had a fling a few years back when I was still teaching. Nothing more than being a bit shitfaced and going to bed together one evening. He has never quite looked at me the same since then. He makes me uncomfortable in the way he puts an arm around me whilst we all drink in the living room; the jealous looks he gives off when I talk to other men. It goes on I'm afraid.

I've never liked this form of behaviour. I've slept with plenty of people in my time because of drunken lust or simply because I wanted to and could. To me, it is often just sex. Nothing more than fun. Men do not seem to share my mentality and this could be why I have never managed to hold down a long term relationship with anyone. Well, it doesn't matter but we had it out with each other on New Years Day and he stomped out.

It was only after then that I realised he had feelings for me but resented me for not having them back. Rather than submitting to his ideas of protection and being his woman, I completely rejected them and had always done so. It hurt his pride. So he made things as difficult as possible with me.

I debated going to Princeton, just dropping in and seeing what had changed. Campus would be shut for the Christmas break but there would be no reason why I could not walk around the offices and see it again. But I did not. I doubt I'd be recognised. Its been four years since I left the university and students and staff alike would have moved on. No it was not that stopping me.

It was the sense of regret and disgust. It was obvious to the faculty when I had to resign that things had been going on with one of the students and myself. That I had broken the rules and got caught. Yeah, that much was clear when I was told to resign or be fired. I was one of the few women to teach at all there and I threw it all away. If I could turn back time now then I would and still be here but I cannot. I have to accept my responsibility. I do what I want, when I want. It does mean that I am accountable for my actions and that I have to live with them.

I make more money now than I dreamed. My work is easier and less stressful. I do not miss having to deal with students but I do miss the nature of my work. There are many regrets and mixed emotions in all of this. I find myself looking back and wondering how things would be if I'd done it differently now.

I'm sending you this letter from New York but I leave for San Francisco tomorrow night. I wrote this from the sofa whilst everyone else had passed out drunk. An empty bottle of wine sits beside me along with an ashtray of stubbed out cigarettes. I cannot curb my addiction to these two vices; indeed I need them more than ever. There is no doubt in my mind that if I'm not an alcoholic then I'm not far off it.

Happy holidays to you Sven.

Yours,

Cassandra

April 1942
London

Dear Sven,

I'm watching her take a nap whilst I write. She fell asleep as we listened to jazz music on the radio in my apartment. It's boiling outside, even on an early summers evening April. Hannah spends even more time than before at my apartment now - she hasn't returned home in almost four days.

You might ask how this came to pass. I started to take your advice on getting to know Hannah better, so we made it a habit of meeting up every second Sunday and spending the day together. This went on for several months during a particularly cold winter, where one needs hope and good company to pass the time. Well, we became closer and closer still as the weeks went by.

Entering the spring, we found the sun slowly delaying its deadline to finish the day. There was more time after work to meet each other and the warmer days encouraged us to spend time in the parks. I dared not take her to the Roxy or any of my previous hangouts. Instead, we preferred each others company, having date days and social time alone as we discussed the idea of my book and what we wanted in the world. Our interactions only continued to strengthen our bond.

So it was one night in early March when we spent a lovely Friday together. Laughing, sharing wine and enjoying each others company, we simply lost track of time. It was only when we realised it was past midnight and the curfews were in effect. An annoyance, and possessing no car, I could not get her home. I insisted that I would take her home in the morning (Roger was away all week on business and would not miss her.) She smiled and simply replied that she was happy to stay with me.

Although I have a spare bedroom, we somehow ended up in my bedroom. She had told me in the past that she prefers to not sleep alone if it is possible, so that she would be reassured of being safe if we had an air raid. In the bed, I found myself holding her in my arms, slowly nodding off to sleep after a lovely day with a woman that I had built a friendship with.

And then she leant over and kissed me once on the lips. Softly and with absolute autonomy. After that, it all becomes a blur but a very romantic blur all the same. We made love twice that evening and then once in the morning. It was the first time since Cassandra where I had made love to a woman and felt something beyond lust. Indeed, I was almost afraid to kiss her again after the first kiss and it was only upon her placing her hand on my chest that I threw caution into the wind.

I feared she would be gone in the morning, or at least cold and off putted by the idea of betraying her husband. But she was there, in the bed, one arm slightly on me as she breathed softly into the pillows. When we made love again that morning, it was sober and intense, eyes looking constantly into each other, smiles and laughter as we continued. I found myself lost in the moment; a moment of sheer bliss shared by the one person I wanted more than anyone else.

That was over a month ago. With Rogers growing absence from her life, owing to reasons I believe we both find suspicious but presently remaining without discussion; Hannah spends an increasing amount of time with me. So far, we have opted to keep our affair a secret. Indeed, you are the only person I have told.

Keep my secrets Sven,

Brian.

May 1942
San Francisco

Dear Sven,

I've started writing a book. Well, I have some early drafts right now but beyond that it is nothing more than an illusion right now. Work has been flat out lately and attention to it is hard. This is because of the war that we have been pulled into.

World news was made on that day in December when Japan attacked Pearl Harbor. America has only ever been involved in one conflict like this before and that was in my lifetime. The idea of this again does not frighten me on any enormous scale since the United States is a committed ally against those who wish to poison liberty and democracy - but still it strikes me as madness that the world can be committed to this conflict still. I know I am a bit older than you and that I have lived through these horrors already but this feels different.

Forgive me but still holding my post with the San Francisco Chronicle I am exposed to the details of war and horror more frequently than those who do not work in my profession. Military guard patrol the streets. The Golden Gate Bridge stands with forts on both sides. The fog, which never fails to disguise the otherwise beautiful bay, hides our troops. The city is heavily guarded. My own issues, whatever they seem to be, are minor compared to the chaos in the rest of the world yet for me it is the other way around. My life, though stable and comfortable for a citizen of my standing, is at best convoluted and difficult at times.

I live alone now. Until recently I had a roommate. Sarah. A doctor of philosophy. She worked at the University, teaching history and literature. She left one morning, explaining that she had cause to return to her parent's home in Crescent City. That was six weeks ago. I haven't seen her since. She sends money through every two weeks for her share of the rent so as of yet I'm not in mind to be annoyed. I privately miss her – she was a great laugh.

I play loud jazz music in the evenings and drink wine whilst writing my articles. I smoke until the early hours of the morning. I frequently desire something other than my work, even though I am committed to it. I still retain the image of my Princeton years, though I do not long for the same attention at this time. Anyway, writing beats ramblings to a crowd of bored pupils. I feel more my own spokesman here.

What do you do these days my friend? Tell me everything.

Yours,

Cassandra

July 1942
London

Dear Sven,

Well it seems we're both serious men at last. Hannah has
moved into my flat. The affair is all out in the open now after it
was revealed that Roger had been sleeping with someone else
whilst on his business trips. Hannah confided in me several times
before it started that she had suspected foul play from him.

It seems her suspicions were confirmed about three weeks ago
when he told her about the affair. It seemed guilt overcame him
in the end. She quietly packed a bag and told him she was leaving
the house for a while to think. She turned up at my doorstep
about an hour later and hasn't left since.

Knowing that we were both just as bad as him does not bother
me. Or her. He lost her – not the other way around. I light a
cigarette and contemplate this as the sun slowly sets over
London. I told her she was welcome to stay for as long as she
needed; she threw herself into my arms and we made love on the
sofa before going to bed – the hour was already late.

Truthfully, I am happy with this. It has actually worked out for
the best. Hannah told me that she was unconcerned about his
infidelity since she has not loved him in a long time. He had
behaved like a jerk and according to her, this was not the first
time she had suspected it.

Sven, how can a man treat a woman such as her so poorly? I'm
appalled and actually pretty angry on her behalf. But I think it is
clear that she'll be here for a while. We spend all our free time

together – my book has even struggled a bit lately because I've been so excited to come home and see her. We're basically an item. Unspoken of yet we treat each other as companions and lovers. It fits the bill.

I'm trying to not get too attached to her because of what happened the last time I opened my heart out to a woman. But she already knows me so well. It becomes hard after crossing that gap to ignore the feelings in my heart. I cannot deny that the feelings I claim to have for her exist – they are very real.

We'll see how this goes but for the first time in a long time, I am happy.

Yours my friend,

Brian.

August 1942
San Francisco

Dear Sven,

How are you getting on? Congratulations on your wife being with child! Will you be relocating or do you plan to stay in Lisbon? I imagine this is the start of something incredible for both of you.

I've had a few changes to my life lately, although it is nothing unexceptional. My housemate Sarah, who vanished one morning to her parents' home in Chino, wrote to me this morning. She is not coming back; her father is dying. I sympathise with her, having lost my own when I was thirty-three. I have decided, upon hearing the news, not to seek out a new roommate. I can afford it and to be honest, I have become used to being on my own. It is an economical way to live.

I shall miss the company but it is her company I believe I will miss. I am used to being alone but she was easy to be around. I'd see her briefly on mornings, occasionally on weekends and often in the evenings. She always paid the rent on time and was lovely when I moved into my first and so far, only apartment in San Francisco. I doubt we'll be seeing each other again; contact has been minimal and until this morning, we had not spoken in three months.

Otherwise, my book is progressing well. I have produced academic pieces in the past but this is a cut above from those days. I focus entirely on fiction. I am writing about the past in a fictional sense; about young students growing up on the east coast. Except it is far from fictional. Mark Twain, a hero of mine, wrote that the 'truth is stranger than fiction but it is because fiction is obliged to stick to possibilities. Truth isn't.' And this is true with my own story that I am now working on.

It is about those students. But it comes from mine own experiences within the academic circle. It details the life of a student and a professor and how the two eventually kill each other. The police investigate and conclude that it was a crime of passion and agreed suicide when it was actually an act of misunderstanding and police failure to see the wider picture. It is allegorical for not reading in between the lines and understanding that things are far from what they seem.

Work on this book started several months ago; I have already written out a beginning, middle and end, with the intention of publishing it in the next month. I have my name and position within a leading company to publish the work; I am confident it will be well received by others without issue. But the true secret to the novel is that it addresses our own past and memories. It holds many references to our days together in Princeton and particularly how my final months were. I think you'll enjoy it.

I want you to know that it'll be the start of several books to come. I have many ideas and wish to put them on paper for the public. I need to do something that is not surrounded by journalism. The nature of journalism is easy; you just have to write what your superiors tell you to write and do it at a fast pace. It does not require a brain – merely a grasp of language and a strong work ethic.

Since my aunt died, I have been alone in the city as far as family connections go but I maintain a strong link to many of the known faces in the city. I often go for lunch with high flying people, spend time in the bars meeting younger men and when I am not doing either of these things, working or sleeping, or drinking. I find few other things providing me with satisfaction in life.

What gives you satisfaction Sven? Family life and being a civil servant in Portugal? I always imagined you'd be leading the government rather than following it. You've never been a strong supporter of Sweden; I find it strange to believe that you follow them now as one of their kind in neutral Portugal. But I can see you wanting to be as far away from war as possible, especially now that you are a father to be. I am lucky to have not been knocked up like so many of the dullard women I know living in this city. I guess I took after my aunt in that respect, although she was a devout catholic with a refusal to remarry after her widowing and I have just been lucky to avoid unwanted children so far.

Don't take my last comment offensively Sven. You know after all, that I respect you greatly.

Yours my dear friend,

Cassandra

October 1942
London

Dear Sven,

I just wrote 4000 words for my book. It might be too much for one day but I am happy with the work so far. It is not even 8 am yet. Hannah is still sleeping in the bedroom and I am already burning through my story. She is really helpful for me with my focus because she has been so supportive over this project. When she found out about my idea she told me to do it. That people were either going to ignore my work or hate it or possibly like it. But there is little point of talking about it if I was not prepared to go through with it.

How are you? What are you doing right now? I can imagine you, walking through the streets of Portugal right now to work office. You've told me how hard you work; is this where you thought you'd be once you finished the PHD? I did not imagine I'd be here – I could not have predicted this myself.

We live in fear. Life is full of reasons to be afraid but right now we're being attacked constantly. The Blitz appears to be a distant nightmare but we still see the Luftwaffe in the skies over London and it gives us all reason to remember that we are on borrowed time. The morale in England is good but there is no doubt about it; we're in consistent danger. Communication between other countries is hard – I'm quite certain that you and I would not be able to converse if it were not for the fact that you work as a civil servant in a neutral country that shares an alliance with England. We would not really be able to talk if you lived in France or Germany.

I feel sorry for the French. I've always liked them and I think they've had it as a nation. It is a shame because they had a beautiful country but now it is divided and split up like a cake. We are lucky to avoid this; Portugal has been better at keeping out of this; we have not but here we are. We're safe for now. Hitler is too busy trying to take on the Soviets – they do not have the manpower to directly invade us anymore. That doesn't mean they cannot bomb us to hell every so often and make us all in fear of being killed without being prepared for it.

I think that we might win this war – because I do not think the Germans are in a position long term to fight off both The Allies and the Soviet Union. Stalin is not going to just hand the USSR over to the Nazis and Germany is not going to back off. Did you ever read Mein Kampf? You do not need to, although I'm ashamed to say my father has somehow gained possession of a copy in his house. I had to look at it for work a few years ago. Hitler makes it very clear in that horrible little book that he wanted to invade the USSR to create space for later generations...but all he'll create it for the dead.

I'm optimistic because I think they'll kill each other and do us the favour of taking action. I do not want to go and fight in this war; I might have to but for now I think I can avoid it. One day we'll be able to go and walk on the beaches in Portugal and laugh this all off. But for now we're stuck with this.

Do you think you'll read my book if I send you a manuscript when I'm done? I think that it'll be done on the first draft in the next six months. Hannah was been incredible in supporting me with this and I cannot begin to thank her enough for supporting me with my dream of trying to be a writer in this world.

Roger is still married to her and people do not really know about us yet. We started earlier this year as I told you; this is not a casual affair. I have stopped sleeping with other women in seedy bars and only want to be with her. I feel for her because Roger is a dull, decaying white man that basically tricked her into his bed and then into marriage. Luckily, they do not have any children so walking away from him was easy enough.

We haven't seriously talked about this yet. We're just having too much fun right now. I was a bit afraid of committing to someone that encourages me originally. After Cassandra I felt concerned to date a woman who I felt so combatable with but Hannah is different. She seems to really be interested in what I do and like me for who I am. She reads a lot and says it is an escape from the reality of missing Denmark and being stuck in England as we're surrounded by our enemies.

She hates the Nazis. I'd say she was a pro-left winger because when I told her my father holds right wing sympathies with how the Nazis conducted their business of expelling foreigners in the 1930s; point of the matter was she was absolutely disgusted. We are two of a kind since she has travelled and likes people in general. That we do not recognise the need to be abusive to people based on where they come from; we judge them on their actions.

So right now we're living together and have been for some time. I do not find other women attractive these days. I definitely have feelings for Hannah. If she tells me tomorrow that she is divorcing Roger for me then I welcome being with her publicly and without shame. She fears that she'll be judged for this but I have assured her that I will protect her from such behaviour.

Your wife is Portuguese right? I think that is lovely because you are with her because you love her. Not guided by nationality or by anything else. Just love. I am openly envious because I wish I could move into that place sooner. Trying to be open about things in England is still quite different from other places. But I am delighted that you are so happy, especially given that the war is taking up much of our time.

Sven, I have to go. Hannah is stirring in the other room and I wanted to get some breakfast ready for her before she gets up. She has to get to work later today but she likes to sleep in for long periods where as I prefer to get up early and do my work before the day truly begins. I feel that way that I have time to focus on my office job whilst feeling that I've at least tried to do something worthwhile in the morning.

You take care Sven, I'll talk to you another time

Brian.

September 1942
San Francisco

Dear Sven,

I published my novel today. We spoke of the idea in letters these past six months and I told you the idea was happening. Well it is on the shelves today. It is a modernist novel for sure. I cannot deny the influence of Woolf, Fitzgerald or Joyce in my work. Every word flew off my fingers and from my typewriter came this story.

It is not my first book, that you know, and it was not difficult to write a story. I managed to go from start to finish on the actual plot within three weeks. Two months of revisions and the work was complete. While it was not difficult to write, it was exhausting and I'm now starting to realise that.

The book has been well received by friends, critics and the press so far. People seem to be excited about it. I did not realise I could write as quickly as I actually did; nor that I was brave enough to discuss this subject in my work. It is the story of students sleeping with each other and how they eventually kill each other in a moment of madness at the end of the story. It is bleak; no doubt of that and not for everyone.

I address my past in it. Our past in some respects. Don't worry, it is entirely fictional and almost all the factual parts of the story have been altered; the only thing you might recognise is the themes of the story. Even the genders have been swapped about to hide the nature of the story. It is pretty autobiographical but borrows a lot of themes from colonial writers like Conrad.

Ah sorry to go on about this – I know you've never been the biggest literature fan but I cannot contain my excitement. Anyway, it is called 'Souls of New York' and it is published under my true name. I prefer not to use a pen name and would rather the world know me for who I am. I've sent you a signed copy with this letter and I hope you enjoy it.

Not much else to say. I had to write the thing after that incident in New York over Christmas and I want you to know that I've done it with the intention of offering some cathartic way of addressing the past and finally being allowed to go into the future.

Yours my friend and happy reading,

Cassandra

November 1942
London

Dear Sven,

I've managed the time to write to you again. It is five am in the morning on a Tuesday and I am due to get up to go work in a couple of hours. I went to bed at twelve but I found myself rising from my sleep around half an hour ago with the urge to write. The same urge that I have been twitching from for the last month or so.

My life seems to be charging by without too much circumstance developing beyond the pleasures of my own world. It feels like I've actually seriously started to enjoy living in London, to call myself a Londoner, to embrace the lifestyle and the culture of this place. In many ways I am actually very lucky to be where I am right now. I find myself wishing I had found this stride in my life sooner but then again it is better late than never that I am finally happy. Things continue to go well at work and even though I am sometimes a bit too keen to leave the office by quitting time I find myself even enjoying my job.

And I owe much of this to Hannah.

The war still rages on around us on the continent, always infiltrating our media and our press each morning and closing at night like an impatient landlord who wants to kick the drunks out. It is impossible to avoid and I feel as if the damage to Europe will be long term after this war has concluded. Things will be different one way or another for the British Empire. The damage has already been done in some of her colonies and even if this war is to be lost by the allies on the mainland, I can envision that this war has changed colonies that even the Axis Powers command. Things will not just go back to how they used to be. Even in Sweden I think change is bound to hold some form. Nothing is set when faced with the river of time anyway, but the world isn't just being altered by the war – it is being transformed by it.

I often wanted to see a world without a British Empire. A world free of such monstrous ambitions to control and 'educate' entire civilisations to its will. I believe that we might actually be witnessing this now. After all, there is no way the imperial empire will preserve after this conflict. The greatest power known to man, the biggest war fleet ever commissioned by our government and controlling enough military might to reign fire over entire countries – ravaged by war, time, debt and idealism. Even if we survive the war, change will happen. I cannot ignore it as I try to sleep at night – the days of imperialism are numbered. Time eventually makes short work of everything.

Yours,

Brian

December 1942
San Francisco

Dear Sven,

I hope this letter reaches you in time to wish you a happy Christmas. I saw the photograph of your child – what a beautiful baby you are blessed with. I'm not sure where you're spending Christmas but I've directed this letter to your address in Portugal. I'm in San Francisco this Christmas; decided to not bother heading home this time. The east coast is my home these days.

I've found that my book might be what we call a sleeper hit. That is to say that the literary press of San Francisco considers it to have 'some fine writing in it but that it is unfulfilled.' Basically, it means that they hated it but that it wasn't considered terrible by the public. I mean, let's just say the opinions were mixed. I did not know how to present it really. I just published it and hoped people would read it.

It seems this was not the way to go about publishing a book. Giving it to you straight, I'm a risk of being forgotten about within the next couple of weeks, if not sooner. The publishing game is hard and people have implied to me that I'm more suited to editing than creating. Nevertheless, there were some who liked it and praised my work as being part of the late modernist movement. One reviewer even addressed me as the next great feminist writer. I don't know how to take that last bit.

The reception has not been unkind but it has not been warm. How do I feel? Unconcerned. It is easy to write a book for me. All I had to do was take elements of my own past, blend them into a narrative of fictional but believable characters and sell them to people who could relate to them. I must confess that I did not spend long on the book, with little time dealt to the writing and a few weeks on the editing process.

In time, maybe this little book will be understood differently. I attended several press releases and interviewers on the nature of the story. A recurring theme asked by readers was about my past in Princeton. I have to give the same reply over and over; that I would not be discussing my past career in Princeton or my sudden departure from the university in late 1937. You can relax; you're not in it and neither is your old roommate. Although you might find references to things you like in the story. That the topic was off limits and any non-fictional association to the author and the characters is purely coincidence.

This has led me to some issues in promoting the book as I am now wondering if indeed I should have addressed the themes of promiscuous sex in my novel; it is something you gain a reputation for quite easily as an older woman. But the book is written. Names were altered and entire details changed. Indeed, the only connection this writer shares with her book is the certain theme of how to not live a lifestyle with students. I mention influences to be Austin, Rand, Mrs Fitzgerald and Wolfe to name a few. I am purposely cryptic about this because the influences of other writers are unimportant – the story is important. I am capable of drafting a story from my own brain without the help of others.

When I published the book, I did so through work. Relatively easy to do. My superiors were happy to promote the book and my boss even liked it, although he suggested that I spend more time exploring the ideas of high society and the sexual themes behind it instead of focusing the relationship on several characters and their social interactions in New York. But they were happy to promote a female journalist who has a strong legacy in literature on her premier novel. I've sold several thousand copies but not as many as they'd like. I didn't write the book for them or for you. I wrote it for me.

I'm not interested in what people think.

Or I pretend not to be. I would have liked people to see it for what it is. Simply young students and teachers being lost in the world and not knowing how to relate to each other without blurring their own guidelines. Something that I think each one of us has struggled with at some stage. It dawns upon me that whenever a book is written from the heart by a writer, the public will do all they can to analyse it to their wits end.

My greatest frustration is that my readers have simply missed the point of what I was attempting to do in the book. It is not that I'm displeased with my book; only that it could have been better. Or different. Or not at all and attempted something safer. Something that could be easier to market Upon rereading it, at least.

I did not write the thing for money. I did it for myself and I make no bones about that to people who ask me questions. Those people who are determined to read between the lines and find things that simply are not there. Some of them have been listening to Hemingway and his iceberg theory for too long. A concept I admire in writing but not one I used in this novel.

So, there you have it. 'Souls of New York' is out and available to buy. You can read into it however you like. It is an easy read and I think you'll get through it in an afternoon. I will be returning to journalism for the time being and writing directly on the war effort which America is involved in. Pearl Harbor was just over a year ago now and we need every word to count in helping the country to go forward. My work is there until I can get time to prepare a second novel. Because I think I will attempt a second novel when the occasion is correct. Just not yet.

Over a thousand words later and I have not even asked you how your wife is in the aftermath of your first born. Then again, I have always been a selfish woman in that regard. The truth is I never worry about you Sven; you've always been the strongest of the strong.

Have a wonderful Christmas,

Cassandra

January 1943
San Francisco

Dear Sven,

Shitty weather over here! How are things in the land of Portugal? I saw some excellent photos of your garden and the terrace with your wife and young child! I think she makes a fantastic pairing to you Sven. I'm sure the future holds good things for all of you.

Now that my book is out and we're back at work writing on the war effort, I have to admit that I am lacking in clarity about what I'm going to do next. My desire to focus on myself is paramount but burning the candle at both ends is exhausting. With my progression in the company, I am now considered a senior journalist.

With all of that, I do think that I'm managing alright. You seem to be doing better than me these days but we both know why. You're not fucked up like I am. You seem to be relaxed and easy about everything. It all seems to just blend in with you – there is no cause for stress or upset. How is not smoking or drinking for you right now? Have you found it hard to not cave in? I started consuming several packets of cigarettes per day whilst drinking at least one bottle of wine a day.

This was really just a quick note to tell you that I've been holding up. Still no strong relationships on the horizon. Managing very well with living on my own – I am purely my own boss and it is brilliant. In our office, I am usually left to my own devices and allowed to pursue my work, both personal and professional.

Tell me about your child. Is it a healthy girl? I hope so. I cannot imagine how excited you must be for the days to come. To think

you were once a young and inexperienced man in a university –
now on the way to higher things in your career and the joys of
fatherhood.

Tell me all you can in your next letter about the coming
months Sven.

Yours darling,

Cassandra

February 1943
London

Dear Sven,

Disaster has struck! I've lost my drafts of my novel – all of it is bloody gone.

I was on a train back from York after spending a weekend covering a story put out by our office, when I left the bloody thing in a café, just before leaving the place to come home. Back in London, I contacted the café and they do not have any idea what happened to it. No idea at all.

So that's it. All that hard work – wasted.

I do not know if I'll restart the thing or if my ideas are simply that of a dreamer. Either way, I feel depressed and gloomy about my future ambitions. Fed up is putting it mildly. So I guess I'll go get drunk this evening, even though it is a Sunday night with work early tomorrow – honestly I could not care less right now. It's only three now and the sun is already setting on this dreary day in February.

I'm royally fucked off.

Brian.

March 1943
London

Sven,

Well I've started again with the book.

From scratch. The only thing I did not leave behind was a small blue notebook that luckily contained some of the key information for my characters. I can use that to frame the majority of the story until I figure something out with fixing the plot up. The real issue is shaping the story to its previous form.

What annoys me is that all is takes is one slip up and you can end up back to the start without any hope of getting where you need to be. It was with that understanding and a conversation with Hannah recently that allowed me to have some serious clarity in where my novel was going. Where it can still go.

Hannah told me about something she read in a magazine a while back. Ernest Hemingway once lost all of his notes and stories on a train when he too was young and starting out in the world of writing. Before he'd broken into the world in the way he did; he managed to be in my situation. Hemingway did not give up – only three years ago, he published *For Whom the Bell Tolls*. And he is far from alone in making it after a horrendous set back.

So, around two weeks ago, after being depressed and moping around the house on the weekends, I sat down at my desk and began to rewrite my story. I must say that a good chunk of this was because of Hannah. She told me, in no uncertain terms, how unmanly I was at risk of becoming. That my attitude had gone from 'put up or shut up' to feeling sorry for myself and drinking too much.

It was with this conversation that I knew she was right.

Going back on the last two weeks now, I've made good progress. Four chapters of my book are now written and with roughly two-hundred words to go before I'll take a break and then look at the rewrites – well I am happy. Really happy so far. This does mean that my publication will be delayed but it is at least better than moping around the flat.

In order to focus on getting this work done, I've turned the spare bedroom into an office so I can focus on my writing. I've placed an old desk, coupled with a few helpful items in the room and I keep my work in there at all times. Can't risk taking it out again and having the same problems. I've installed a new rule of leaving the manuscript at home, with a notebook that I now keep on me at all times.

Rewriting the book was initially soul destroying, but with time and patience, along with hard work, I'm confident that I can make it better than it was to begin with. I owe much of this to the encouragement of Hannah, who has forced me to either get back on with it or to just forget about being a writer altogether. The former was not an option to me; so here we are.

Yours Sven,

Brian

April 1943
San Francisco

Dear Sven,

Well this place is like an occupied zone. That is literally all I can probably tell you about the military presence in the bay area.

How are you anyway? Keeping safe despite all the war in Europe? I often feel for you, living in a country like Portugal, for yourself but the benefits of being from a neutral country and living in another – I don't think you need to be concerned about the political landscape in your town. You're a diplomat, I'm a journalist. I'm paid to be critical about people but I will not mess about with your office. Christ, politics is about as dull as a math teacher. I'm sure you'd agree.

I've taken a semi-permanent lover in the city. We've been sleeping together for a few months now; met at a bar I visited on the off-chance for a quick drink before turning in early for the night. It seems that statements like 'one drink' or '30-minute pit-stop' are pretty fatal to my kind. Anyway, we met that night. You'll be pleased to know that this one is older than me. Salesman, works in the city, divorcee and has two kids from his failed marriage. He is a bit dull once you get to know him and always talks about his work.

To be honest, I might break it off. He is in the older stages of life, surpassing me by around twelve years. Wants to resettle and probably thinks I'm his ticket to retirement. Says he admires a girl that works and puts herself first. I admit to not exactly being Dorothy Thompson but I found his tone pretty condescending. I'm a part-time public intellectual, not some café girl. To be honest, I sleep with him for my pleasure and because it has been quite a few months of abstinence prior to meeting the Salesman.

I seriously do not want a long-term man. My work is my life and I roll with the motions of being a journalist in a city that is thriving. We've well and truly shaken off the great depression as we now call it because of the war effort. The world always needs journalists and I'm bloody good at what I do. I actually make more money than him in the long term since he is self-employed; I have my salary and life. But it is nice to be taken out occasionally by the Salesman. He's good looking for an older man, despite the slight greying hair and developing beer gut.

But he is so fucking dull Sven. I drink a lot when we go out and often we become dizzy by nine in the evening. You cannot hold my lifestyle here without gaining a reputation of being a boozer; I'm viewed as pretty manly compared to many of the women in town, although I couldn't care less. They can be sheep all they like. I live my life on my own terms.

Work is the same. In full swing with the war effort and drafting up piece after piece, week by week. A journalist from the New York Times interviewed me recently about my book. I had to admit that I was excited to talk about it, but the questions about my past and my sudden departure from Princeton came up, even though the book is not connected to that period of our lives. I did not take it well but reluctantly finished the interview despite several 'no comments' being issued to the journalist.

Otherwise, life continues here and we make the best of a bad situation. The war is dragging on but we've had time to get used to it now. Just disgusted about the behaviour of forcing Japanese-Americans from their homes. I do not agree with this legislation and frankly I think it's safe to say it is immoral. Order 9066, they are calling it. Another glorious piece of racism in American history.

I hope you're keeping well and that you are enjoying the life in Lisbon.

Yours,

Cassandra

June 1943
London

Dear Sven,

They say the trick to a good novel is to be punchy and get to the point as fast as possible.

I say they're regrettably right. I have just had to scrap a lot of the first draft in the book. Over the last few weeks I have spent hours editing the thing, working late and barely sleeping. But I'm happy to say I've cut out the mess and got into the heart of the beast. At 350 pages, I think it is fair to say the book is coming close to ready.

Or at least it is actually a book now with characters and a plot. Not bad given that three weeks ago it was less of a book and more of a bloody mess. And definitely not bad given that only four months ago I lost the sodding manuscript and had to begin my work again from scratch.

Hannah has been instrumental in changing me from a lost sheep to a functioning writer who devotes time and energy to his craft. She is the deciding factor in helping me create the book. Offering me so much support on the book, encouraged me, read drafts, spent hours telling me not what to write but how to write... In the end, I really owe it to her. If the book is to be a best seller or a flop remains to be seen but I'm unconcerned. Writing it and publishing it is the goal. Because of her support, that means it is happening.

And I end on a positive note. That despite the war, all this rot getting us down, that we are actually happy. We are living and getting by, managing with it all. I have hope for us Sven. I truly do.

Be well my friend,

Brian

July 1943
London

Dear Sven,

Why is it so hard to write a book? Things seem to constantly interfere with my life. Work, family meetings, the war, life. It all seems to slow the process down.

I had a rare meeting with my father recently. I went to his house in Hampshire on a Sunday. He owns a huge house in the countryside. Makes it hard to believe I came from this type of upbringing when I look at my own working-class lifestyle.

I have always suspected my father of holding sympathy for the Nazis in Germany. He frequently spoke of wanting to visit Berlin in the 1930s and has never held high regard of Jews. I owe much to him; he funded me in America; helped me in Saigon and made sure I could get home safely.

I have always hated to admit that I am related to the man and am reluctant to talk about him. At 64, he is still an important figure in the law community of England although he spends much of his time these days in his house, entertaining guests and occasionally guest lecturing. His view points have always been on the right and he has been known to postulate frequent ideas in stark contrast to that our current cabinet. He would prosper under Nazi Germany because of these tendencies and it disgusts me.

I attended the lunch because I am somewhat in my father's debt. He has agreed to promote the draft I am working on among my colleagues, although he considers the literature worthless. My older brother followed into the firm he helped build. My sister was the next in line to hold office, despite how my father's feelings about women – he sees her as a steely bitch that can destroy anything she opposes. Given that my father and I have never shared eye to eye, yet despite his public image for being a family man with his two older children and a hidden son; he allowed me to pursue my love of literature, partly out of not wanting to spoil his socialite image.

He has never really liked me as a son. I drank early, smoked, and frequently hung out with characters that he would not allow into the house. My older brother and sister replicated his statements, hung out in exclusive clubs whilst I showed no interest in his firm and only wanted to be a writer – something he felt that was the dream of leftist intellects and fools. As my siblings fulfilled his legacy, he could not see the harm in having a weak link that did not cause trouble and just wanted to be left to his books.

So, I never caused trouble. He allowed me to exist, although he never actively approved. It is a tolerated relationship because we are family and without this link, I'd have nothing to do with him. When I told him, I was working on my book, he immediately offered to give me money to promote it – he never asked what it was about. I did not tell him about my love life, work or how I have managed to avoid the drafts and conscription. This was because he was able to get me a job in a company where I am needed and cannot just be sent to fight in the army. He knows about the work I do because he knows the board of directors on our company.

And he did not ask about my love life because he simply does not want to know. I did not once mention Hannah. He is aware that I disapprove of his anti-Semitism and closet support of the Nazi party. We are father and son. That is all.

Lunch went alright. My father spent much of his time sitting on the balcony of the house, talking about the need for addressing the Jewish problem whilst Clive and Patricia agreed like whipped dogs. In silence, I smiled and pretended that this was all okay whilst I toyed with my food. I had never felt so disgusted with my brother. At eleven years my senior, he looks down on me as the dreamer whilst he prepares to amass the legacy that my father has built. He sees himself as the future of a great and noble vision – I suspect that the only reason he tolerates me is because of our father.

My father was helped from the table by the maid and taken to the bathroom whilst I excused myself to get another drink. I've never been truly comfortable with house servants, preferring to take responsibility for myself. I also had to get away from my siblings for a moment. Clive had continued to talk about how if we can afford to, we should make peace with Germany to prepare for what he describes as a growing 'red threat in the east.' My father returned and only then asked me if I was able to make ends meet in the city.

I had, as I previously mentioned, been in my brother's flat for the first few months back in England. I had since moved to a place closer to work and the parks. My brother was rarely there; he used the place for little more than a base to work and then went to his house on the weekends. I had to get out of there quickly and rented a place using my wage from my firm; much to my father's disapproval. I sought to shake off my privileged roots and attempted to be my own man, not living in a shadow of racism and corruption where status and money talks.

I took the train home that evening and prepared for my working week. I do not know when I shall see all the family together again; probably my sister's birthday in August. Too soon.

I have always spoken openly of you on this subject and it pains me that several years later, almost nothing has changed. They are products of the empire, a dying breed and frankly disgust me, even if blood connects us. If not for this connection, I do wonder if we'd even share a connection or if I'd simply see them from afar, opponents on the ideological battlefield.

Yours my friend,

Brian

August 1943
Sacramento

Morning Sven,

I'm standing on a terrace in Sacramento, looking across the city right now. I've taken a few days off from San Francisco. Needed it; the work load in the office has been a bit much lately. Being here is a welcomed relief.

Who the hell are we going to kill next in this crazy war that we're slowly winning? I needed to have a break from that too, although it is true that I have not got involved in the conflict like so many of our countrymen. I've never even fired a gun before, although I grew up around the woods of Maine where bears are a common thing.

When I was fourteen, still in Maine, I lost my virginity to a local boy who delivered mail to my parents' house. It was one afternoon by a lake when no one was around and I had found myself attracted to him for some time. We went cycling on a Sunday after he invited me to hang out. It was painful and now feels like a distant memory. I saw him twice more that summer before I left to go to New York with my family. We never spoke again. I cannot even recall his name now.

I never told anyone about this. He was almost three years older than me but we held the same level of maturity because women always mature faster than men. I kissed him first, once hard on the mouth, then he took me in his arms and we clumsily fell on each other in the grass.

Looking back at this now, nearly forty years later, I think about how my life has changed and the death of innocence that came with the summer when I fell in the grass with the mail boy.

Memory is indeed a stranger and who I was in that period of time is a stranger to whom I am now. I had no concept of war or the blood that could follow. Nothing beyond being some quiet, smart kid who liked her books.

Unlocking that lust for boys corrupted me. But ultimately, I corrupted myself and others in my actions. I became the true thing that did this because I believe I was made to do it. By the time I attended college, which my father could afford to send me to, I'd slept with about eight guys. Most of the girls in my dorm were virgins. I viewed this as the start of my life and when I began to go against the grain.

It made me a social outcast and threw me off the wagon that many of the prudish girls rode. It was also why I probably came to prefer the company of men so early on. I never brought guys home to the dorm because I did not want the judgement of these girls. I kept a quiet life and focused on my studies whilst they were staring at boys but were terrified to go near them. By the time I had finished my studies, I was able to go directly into a teaching position whilst I worked on my PhD in literature.

Many of those girls became housewives. I built a life worth living. I decided when I studied there that I never wanted to be like them. My only true friend was a girl called Hazel, who I used to go running with and talk about books. She was wonderful and we even moved into together in our third term. She married this jerk off prick who used to treat her like shit. I told her to leave him numerous times. The guy eventually killed her with a chopping knife and it was the day my love for the human race died.

I attended her funeral and cried for a long time afterwards. It was another moment of when I felt my innocence die. It was the day the girl in me died and along with it the interest in ever chasing a marriage.

I never talk about my feelings to anyone but you really. I hold you as my most valued friend in the world because you know me. That I can tell you anything. I never talk about this because I do not trust people. But I trust you Sven. You are the single most important person in the world to me.

And I have always adored you darling.

Cassandra.

October 1943
London

Dear Sven,

Summer has finally passed into the background, like a faded photograph of a long-gone relative that no one really remembers and we forget how we ever coped with the cooler weather, whilst nostalgically craving a warmer time we barely appreciated at the time. This is the autumn and it is far from divine. I made the mistake of going to my office this morning without a coat and paid the price by shivering on the train ride home.

Despite the cold, and the coming gloom, I have some good news – the book is finished! I managed to get the last of the editing done three days ago. With this mammoth of a project finally complete, I can submit it to a publisher. This is actually the easy part; my father, despite his lack of interest in any literature, let alone mine, has contacts that he has sourced. Perks of being his son I believe.

So, I've given them a copy and I await the outcome. I might need to make some adjustments to the story but otherwise I believe that I've revised the text so precisely that I do not believe a single word is wasted. An exhausting procedure but a necessary one since it is the only way to ensure that every word serves the writer and his craft.

I've been an inconsistent writer before. I sometimes sit for hours after work, wine and cigarettes in tow, pouring my soul into the pieces that I conceive. Then I will sometimes not write for days. This was for years the nature of my work ethic. Did I dare call myself a writer then? It is one of the few things that once I started to enjoy, I found that I do it so well. Indeed, it is one of the few things I truly love, regardless of whatever mood I am in at the time. I find the rhythm, the pace and the tone then I just go for hours and hours. It helps. Above all else, I do not feel like I have much choice about doing. It has become a need, not a want.

When I was at school, I was told to feel small, to believe in certain things without any question at all. I was led to believe that I was a no-hoper; that I was going to achieve little. The problem child at school who drifted off the map some years later, occasionally to resurface and bring up faint memories like those distant summer days we try to recall in the darkest nights of the winter. I started to reject this idea of what I ought to be when I reached 16 and urged my father to send me to Princeton. I knew and had known for a while by this point that I should study the works of great writers. I know and have always known that literature was my first love.

And now my first book is about to be published. I've finally achieved something that I've wanted after all these years.

Yours,

Brian

November 1943,
San Francisco

Dear Sven,

I wish you well in Lisbon right now. You've been lucky to stay out of the war. One country that you work in is neutral; the country of your birth also neutral. In many ways, you've always been the silent, neutral type. Never raising your voice too loud but always remaining an essential device in keeping two sides from clashing and killing each other outright. I think that is the quality in you I have always admired the most. The remarkable level of restraint and clear head.

You know that the weather in Northern California is rubbish when you wake up and find that it has done nothing but rain all day, causing the air to feel even colder than normal. At least, it gets that way in the late fall. Mark Twain might have said that 'the coldest winter he ever spent was a summer in San Francisco.' Times like this, I tend to agree with him.

Not much has changed here. We still have a pretty huge military presence because there is a lot of fear about being attacked by the Japanese. That and this is a military hotspot, since we're a coastal city, staring into the eyes of the great ocean. Hard to think that on the other side of this body of water is 'our enemy.' The Japs do feel that way; Operation Torch, the taking of Sicily and so forth might have been enormously successful in sending the Axis powers packing in the Mediterranean. The people in San Francisco don't really think about this when they're staring at potential Japanese bombers on the horizon.

I've been flat out lately; working on the war effort in our department and churning out piece after piece on the morale of the city. My boss has headhunted me to be on a project of interviewing Harry Truman in the next couple of months. Competition is aggressive to get the part and plenty of my male colleagues are already commenting that it is no place for a woman in our day and age. Fuck that – I'll prove them wrong.

I mean, why can't I do the job? I've been stuck in San Francisco for what feels like a lifetime – the last time I got out of here was to go to Sacramento for a few days. The cold air in Washington will do me some good compared to the rain over here. Haven't been sleeping a whole lot lately, owing to the heavy cycle of eat, work, sleep and repeat. Loads of things on my desk each day. I should not be ungrateful that I get the work; I'm one of the few women in my department. I guess what helps is that I am damn good at my job and everyone knows it; it is not possible to ignore me when I can churn out pieces faster than my male colleagues can think. Anyway, it is old news. I dealt with this often enough in Princeton. Do you recall our rant in a student bar about this with those young conservatives when we first met?

Drinking and smoking on the evenings helps. I suspect I get through about two packs a day. Some of my more strident colleagues are anti-smoking and create such a fuss when you light up in the office. Liberals mostly, being pathetic and looking for something to get self-righteously upset about. I'm pro-women's rights in the work place and in society, obviously, but there is something unattractive about this type of complaining in a man.

Since you speak French (among five other languages isn't it?) 'Vouloir le beurre et l'argent du beurre.' They really need to get over themselves and stop being so whiney about things. I will continue to smoke in the office and if it causes them offence then too bad. I get enough grief from them anyway.

So I'm pushing for this opportunity to attend a political conference in Washington DC in a few weeks by writing a proposition to my boss; with questions to generate curious answers for the Chronicle. People in San Francisco are interested. This country is so vast and wide that it is difficult to comprehend that we're governed by a district almost three thousand miles away; yet we're the first line of attack on the mainland against the Japs. It is a bit of a scary thought and thus we have a job to do; even if there is a colossal amount of water between us and them.

I pause to find my cigarettes and start to quickly read over my letter to you. It seems until now I have forgotten to mention to you that I broke it off with the Salesman. We were actually seeing each other since roughly mid-February and he was nice enough. Knew how everything worked in the bedroom and not an unattractive older man. But he was looking for something a bit longer term. I have no idea if I can produce children anymore but frankly it is something that does not interest me even if I could. His life was at risk of becoming lonely, being a divorcee and all. Mine is far from lonely, even though I am now alone.

He reminded me of a man who wanted to control me; to tell me not to work and to just enjoy my life. My life is my work and I enjoy it absolutely. I like rising to the challenge and proving my lot in life. I have inherited this from my father, who encouraged my love of literature and writing. A radical old liberal. In many ways, the Salesman reminded me of too many men I know. They are either puppy-dog-eyed for me or telling me that I need to slow down.

At any rate, I'm pushing for this assignment on Washington and I need to get back to drafting my proposal. It is due in a few hours and I have to get it finished if I stand a chance of towering over the whiney liberals in the office. A third cigarette for good measure as one of them attempts to eat a sandwich two desks down makes me feel better.

But again – I've taken up the bulk of my letters with rants. You must be sick of it by now. Knowing that one of your old friends from eons ago is writing to you, only to complain about her life. I'm grateful that you put up with my ramblings darling.

You'll always have my friendship so long as I have yours,

Cassandra

December 1943
London

Dear Sven,

Happy Christmas my friend. I'm staying in the city for the week, looking after Hannah. She has become unwell with the flu and I'm going to take care of her until she improves. Rationing makes it difficult to provide any decent gifts but she made me a sweater from sheep wool; I got her two books (Picture of Dorian Gray and A Tale of Two Cities) that she has longed for an age over.

All in all, we're going strong together. Very strong. I couldn't be happier. My book is about to be published, I am in love with Hannah and we're safe. Well as safe as we can be, in London. Safe as houses is an English expression, I've always been fond of, but true safety is in the bomb shelters.

I find it madness to think that almost thirty years ago, Germans and English lads were playing football in France; now here we are. Marooned on our island and fighting what some might call a mere extension of the First World War. Maybe so. Or maybe our failure was in not getting the poison out after we were finished with Germany. This time we will have to do better. The war is turning. Campaigns in Africa have seen to that.

I cannot help but feel that all of this is too good to be true. That something will come along and spoil all the great moments we are having. Rationing won't be it; the bombs won't do it. I think me being away from her will do it. I cannot help but feel that our time is running out – that we're on borrowed time now. Like all of this is simply the calm before a truly terrifying storm that lurks somewhere across the English Channel.

I fear being sent to the front. So far my father, for all his faults, has prevented that. My job, in the firm, working tirelessly as a journalist for the morale has kept it at bay. But my father is an old man of declining influence; a member of a generation that has served its time. He has little relevance or power these days, despite his legendry status in the civil courts. No, I fear our time in this bubble of safety is running out.

But for now, I intend to enjoy Christmas. I can hear her stirring in the bedroom. These days, I often rise early to work on pieces for work so I can get home early in the evening to spend my limited time with her. Our evenings are precious and few, especially when all able hands are required to support the country as well as we can.

My dear Sven, I hope you have a wonderful Christmas and a happy New Year. Attached to this letter is a signed copy of my book, which is due to be published next month. I wanted you to have an early copy for Christmas. It might be the thing I am most proud of in my lifetime so far. I want to share it with you.

Yours my friend,

Brian.

January 1944
San Francisco

Dear Sven,

I managed to trump all those second-rate journalists in my office by taking a trip, all expenses paid, to Washington this week. I was to cover a press conference given by members of the Roosevelt administration in regards to American foreign policy. This was also to interview Vice-President Harry Truman. Entry into the war will be remembered as the moment on December 7th when the Japanese attacked Pearl Harbor.

I'll say right off the bat that I spent fifteen minutes with the Vice President. Much of the conversations I had at Washington have to be omitted from this letter, but general consensus is that the fight continues. The real hope, Truman told me, was not the success so far but what was to come in the future.

Since we got attacked first, we never had much choice in this. Critics had argued that if we stayed out of the European conflict beyond threats to the enemy and global aid to our allies then we ran the risk of maintaining the deep-seated ignorance of our previous generations.

Others argued that if we got involved then we risked invoking the Nietzschian dictum of turning into monsters when we fight the monsters. Hardly win/win and I sometimes wonder if my opinions and reports are completely rational. It is hard to be coherent. Then again war itself is completely irrational so can you blame me for my confusion?

I spent much of the Friday morning touring the sites of Washington DC. The Lincoln Memorial, which has stood for 22 years now, is by far one of the most impressive features of public commemoration that I have ever witnessed in American history. This is the fourth time I have wandered through the Greek styled temple of the late president and even now pimples gather under the skin of my body as I meet Lincoln's eyes. It has been snowing over the last few weeks in Washington, making the steps to the monument treacherous - upon my return towards the Reflection Pool I almost slipped down the stairs!

Staying in a hotel on New Hampshire Avenue granted the ability to flit back and forth across the city as the week progressed. I honestly think I spent more time sightseeing than working on my piece for the Chronicle. I briefly considered taking a train to New York for the week and making the piece up on mere hearsay but professionalism prevailed and I served my week in the capital city. I know that my time there will lead to the creation of an important article concerning American foreign policy yet all I cared about one Wednesday afternoon in the ice and snow of the east coast climate was simply the desire to return to a past life of roughly a decade past. Sorry to droll on about that - I can't talk about foreign policy in overseas letters right now anyway so you're not missing much on that detail.

I flew back to San Francisco on the Saturday afternoon, arrived home around 5, crashed into bed, fatigued from travel, a ruin by roughly eight and sleeping until midday on Sunday. I considered the whole trip more exhausting than revitalizing. I have better things to do right now than be like this. I worked through Sunday evening and by Monday afternoon was rereading the article in that day's edition of the San Francisco Chronicle.

I cannot say I regret going. The whole thing was pretty insightful and if nothing else, gave me a very useful perspective on how things are developing on the front lines right now, not to mention the long term goals once this year ends. It will, that much is certain.

Yours,

Cassandra

January 1944
London

Dear Sven,

I published my book and it is out. I cannot help but feel when I
read it now that it is not going to be considered an outstanding
masterpiece. It has flaws in it, there are grammar errors. A few
but noticeable. A couple of critics have told me that it is a bit
messy and choppy. But I think the main reason it is not so
successful is because of the war going on and everyone dealing
with that.

It has been picked up and praised by others though for being a
good attempt at a first novel. At 350 pages long and with the
influences of authors we know and love within the lines of the
story, I am proud of it. It is not a bad start for a chap living in war
bombed, rationed London.

Hannah was without a doubt the inspiration to finishing the
book. She helped so much with making sure the story flowed, the
pace was clean and that the characters were people that we could
relate to. I will never be the next Steinbeck or Conrad but the
truth is I do not want to be. I wrote the book for me; because I
had something to say that I could not express in any other way.

People do not stop me on the streets like they do with
esteemed writers and musicians and ask for my time of day. I still
work long hours in the office, writing pieces for the war effort
and continue to make enough to pay the rent. But I have done it.
At least I have finally done something that is worthwhile. That is
a start. It is enough for now. Writing the book was exhausting and
I feel that in the aftermath of its publication, I just want to take a

break from writing and play football for the next six months after work instead of going to my desk.

I did get some high praise from critics; although it was limited and I suspect that it won't last. People, including me, are distracted by the ever-present sense of total war that we face in the country. We are pretty much governed by that and little else. So this won't be a classic piece of literature that we'll remember. I'm no Conrad as I say but I am only just starting in my career as a writer; the great work is yet to begin. Many novelists are unsung individuals who are seldom recognised, never mind remembered. I must keep going with my work and not lose heart.

Thank you for all your help in the draft editing and your feedback. You made a hell of a difference in getting me to continue the book. Hannah was the other force that made me finish it and you'll notice in the opening pages of the book that I thank both of you for helping me get it done. Ultimately I dedicate the book to both of you.

The work is only truly beginning now and I believe my next one will be significantly better. One thing I have learnt from writing this book is that you have to turn up and do it. And that your craft improves with experience and graft.

Yours my friend,

From your published novelist friend.

PART III

February 1944
London

Dear Sven,

More places have been bombed of late. London was attacked a few days ago. Operation Steinbock. We have not had anything this bad since the attacks in May '41. The damage is pretty bad but the total war effort of the country prevents us from falling so easy. This war has taken its toll on us all. It is no secret that we've bombed Berlin and they've bombed London. We all suffer in war.

But it seems that I am yet to experience the worst of it. I picked up news yesterday that was far from welcome. It was a conscription draft, sent from the military. I am to fight in the conflicts to come. In fear of this letter being read by the authorities, I cannot say anymore about my involvement in the war but it seems the time has come for me to drop my pen and pick up a gun.

I knew that this was going to happen. That my luck had to run out eventually. I am one of the few young men I know who has escaped being assigned a role in the army so far. I have no idea what will happen to me now. I am still processing the information that causes vomit to be swallowed back as I think of my future. I've always known that my position in my firm was on borrowed time; there was only so long that I could avoid this.

It was a surprise and only, I have to admit, my father's declining influence in society that kept me away from the conflicts. Legislation was passed in December 1943 that meant all young men had to work in mines and luckily, I was too old to be considered. Too old indeed – still young enough to get killed. When I think about getting killed now, I realise that it could have happened anytime. Wrong place, wrong time when a bomb fell, a misguided step and a fall down a flight of stairs, heart failure from the countless cigarettes I've smoked since I was fourteen. You're never too old to get killed in some freak accident or by German design.

I don't resent anyone for this news. We are at war and my help is needed. I am willing to go and fight in the name of my country. Not because I love my country dearly but because Hitler has to be stopped. We have to do everything we can to destroy this madman and his cohorts. If that means I have to get shot at and die in the process then that is what has to happen.

Hannah absolutely resents my fatalism towards this and we've had a slight falling out over it. It is not that I disagree with her; there is nothing good about war or slaughter. Murder is amoral and death is final and democratic, yet it is hesitant if we do not provoke it. I stand the risk of provoking it a lot in the coming months or maybe even years. I do not want to make her hate me and indeed I love her so much that this is why I am willing to go without protest.

I have been lucky enough to avoid all of this for now. A minor thought in the back of my skull asks how this could have happened. Did someone hate my book? Does Roger resent me that much that he wants to kill me and get away with it? Or is it simply the case that we are at war and I must do my part, even if I do not want to?

I won't second guess that last bit. Despite my fantasies and good story lines I could milk into a second book sometime, the answer is clear. We're all in the wrong place right now. Like a bomb that falls in the night on a house full of school children who can barely read or write; never mind understand the disgust of being an adult and feeling hatred towards a nationality they have never met because they're simply too young to understand.

I understand why this has happened. We are at war and in war no one is safe. And there are times when the call is given, then one must be brave and answer it. I do not want to go. I do not want to leave Hannah. I love her and I am sorry that I caused a fight with my stoic nature. But I must also attempt to be brave now. This might be the end of me but I have to be brave for both of us.

I know little more right now than my immediate conscription. I doubt I'll be at liberty to tell you more for a long while ahead. But it is clear to me that the days of sitting in the office, working on behalf of the state are over. My help now is in picking up a gun and trying not to get killed. I do not think there is anything noble in dying like this, but the harsh reality of it is that we have no choice but to fight the fascists this way.

I therefore end this letter by telling you that I am resigned to my fate. But that I will not fall so easy. I have a life to live, books to write and a woman to love. So, with that in mind, I intend to return to the shores of England when this is all over an continue my life with Hannah.

I will be brave for both of us.

Yours,

Brian

April 1944
San Francisco.

Dear Sven,

When I write to you now, I find myself wishing that instead I could open my mouth and say words to you instead. I find myself aware that we are countries apart, beyond waters and facing very different realities. Mine is that my country is about to enter a conflict of which, as a journalist and war correspondent I am not at liberty to discuss in this letter. Yours, having kept a stern neutral hand in the war, has managed to avoid involvement beyond that of being passive land for the Axis powers to stroll back and forth through.

It seems that we both stand at opposite ends of the spectrum of the war without actually being engaged into open conflict with the enemy. The United States, with its isolation and Portugal with its enduring neutrality. I think about this and our relationship between each other. I long for an end to the conflict, to wander the streets of Berlin and Paris again, yet I find myself fearing that once I do return to Europe it will indelibly changed to the world I once knew. (I say that I shall return with such conviction because I know that the Allies will triumph in this war eventually.)

San Francisco is my home now and I have come to love it. The city streets are familiar and pleasant, the people are delightful and the culture vibrant. In many ways I am not certain I can ever return to New York. Even if I did, it is unlikely I would derive my old pleasures from it. It exists in my mind as an imperfect memory fashioned by desire and pleasure. I cannot recall anything beyond the positive memories at this point and as such I know it is a selective detail of my life – San Francisco holds a sense of realism and value beyond that of New York. It exists to me in the material world.

Things are going to get ugly in the conflict with the Germans. That much is clear and that much I can easily tell you right now. I know enough about the fighting in Africa to know that we can win in this conflict against the Axis powers if what we plan to do in the next stage of the war works. Again, beyond this I am not at liberty to discuss. I can only hope that we, in our hopes and optimistic wishes, are proven right.

I often, in my quieter, reflective moments, question why we do not examine this current time with a greater analytical perspective. The Germans' are not monsters and the Japanese, who've taken plenty of swings at the United States since this war started are human beings and far from the beasts we've invented to justify our own actions. We are just humans, running with machines of chaos and murder, burning each other into the brink. Sometimes I stop and remember that at its nexus, this is all we are or will ever be with regards to warfare.

Yours
Cassandra

April 1944
London

Dear Sven,

I've always loved taking walks in the countryside. I spent today with Hannah in Richmond Park. We had some wine, several sandwiches and then spend the afternoon watching the clouds move across the sky. We lay together, her head against my shoulder, just watching, existing within our own bubble. We were briefly but completely untouched by time. It was a beautiful spring morning and the weather was starting to perk up at last. I've always loved April, even when the showers lingered. The day was perfect and we discussed all manner of small things. My book, our plans once things improved in England and the lives we want to leave. I'm getting a bit wiser since our Princeton days I'm prepared to admit that now but I'm feeling like a new aged man.

I love her. I actually think that I might have finally found something in my life that gives me some purpose. My drive is renewed and I feel far more optimistic now than I ever used to. We're lovers - and moving in the right direction. I feel invincible today. Like I have regained control of my life. Today I know that I am the man whom I want to be.

After the sun sank below the hills, we concluded our day by going to dinner in a restaurant. It was truly a magnificent experience for the both of us. I saw an ocean of ideas, passions and beliefs in Hannah. Things I'd not seen in a woman for a very long time. We spoke of poetry, idealism, our love of Morris, Shakespeare, and Wordsworth. But we also found common ground in our political ideals. And we even managed to make the banal topic of cricket enjoyable by laughing at the game we witnessed in the park whilst we drank our wine.

This is it my friend. My life is finally starting to matter.

I just hope I do not die when I'm sent to the front. I leave next month and days like this help me forget the coming storm.

Yours always,

Brian

May 1944
San Francisco

Dear Sven,

How are you getting on? I am sorry that there has not been much news from me lately – things have been hectic in California. So much is going on here right now and its very hard to put everything into context. I know there are things that you want to tell me but since I've heard little from you, you can hear from me.

I've been very stressed lately. We've been working around the clock, promoting the American war effort and attempting to maintain morale. We're an isolated country in many respects. Most Americans are not following the war the same way that the Europeans or Asians do. It is far from our doorstep. Even Pearl Harbor, so long ago, was miles away from the mainland. It simply does not seem to apply to the normal life in California.

Having said that, we're no strangers to the word conflict. We've seen enough blood shed with the Spanish, less than fifty years ago. We're a liberalised state compared to Texas or Utah. We still continue to marginalise half our citizens. I know you've never been the greatest fan of fags but we both agree that they should be treated the same as ordinary citizens. I hope that this kind of enlightenment comes to America before my time is through. A nation that continues in this form of self-sabotage is a lost nation.

By the standards of the next generation, I'm probably a closet homophobe and a racist; by the standards of today I'm considered a radical. I suppose it always depends on the context. People might later accuse Conrad of being a racist. He's not. Simply put, he is a product of his time and a critic of colonial power.

So here I am. An aging woman, complaining about the world she lives in. I'm part of an apathetic society, slowly changing. Using Burkian notions of change, I realise that our world is changing but not in the direction that it needs to. That's where I am at right now in my life. A life of reflection, regret and wishful thinking but knowing that we are united against fascism. Well, a European fascism.

It is this type of hypocritical nature is what will kill us as a nation. We are failing our minorities and still placing white people at the top of the table. History will judge us harshly. But I am a journalist, here to convince people that we are not a fuck-up of a nation and that we're actually on the side of right.

You'll forgive me for this rant of a letter –I've been drinking heavily after a difficult week at the office. Arguing with my prick of a boss over the right to publish this piece defending Asian culture. He thinks I'm a left winger and an idealist. Well maybe I am. I have not cut ties with the left, although I'm no fucking communist. I don't trust those red bastards. Not a single fucking one of them. They all ought to be shot. I know a thing or two about Stalin and his mob.

This war will change us all further. It might not lead to political enlightenment overnight but it will lead to a better nation in time. But we are going to be judged for our actions in this conflict, there is no doubt of that. I don't know if I believe in heaven or hell but one thing is certain – the next generation will not us consider holier than thou. We are all going to hell in their eyes because we have killed and abused our fellow human beings. That is how they will judge us.

So, I have made my peace with the situation. Our fellow creatures are murdering each other in the name of ideology and it will become worse before it gets better. We are the damned and yet we still fight a noble cause against the scum of humanity. Fascism has to be destroyed. But I recall Nietzsche in these moments. We must be care when we fight the monster lest we too become a monster.

This quotation by a nut job should not be misunderstood. Nietzsche was no Nazi but he has been mistakenly thrown into their camp. I studied the man in my youth – he still turns in his grave over this bastardisation of his work and will for long to come. But he is not around to defend himself and neither will we against the judgement of the descendents whose ancestors we have murdered, tortured and socially segregated to profit for our own idealism.

You'll forgive me if I'm starting to bore you with my letter. I am frequently dealing with my work and by that, I mean the work that pays the rent. Not the work I love. Being a journalist is easy. But it does not mean one is fulfilled.

Sven, I will call an end to this rant here. If you got to the end of this letter, know that you have my emotional gratitude and support for hearing an old friend out when it was needed. If this is the case then know that I adore our friendship.

At the last few words, seven glasses of wine and fourteen cigarettes later, all I have to say is that despite all this time, know that I am grateful.

Yours,

Cassandra

May 1944
London

Dear Sven,

I'm going into France soon. We all are. It is coming.

I recently said my farewells to Hannah and to my family. Patricia, my sister, was not there; she had an 'engagement' that prevented her from being there. It was heartbreaking to say goodbye to Hannah; less so to my family.

My father embraced me when I left – something I do not ever recall him having done before. Truth of the matter is he wrote to the government to petition my removal from the forces and to be kept in London. The petition was declined and I was to go anyway. I think he felt defeated and lost, knowing that his youngest son is probably going to his death. I suspect that his weariness had more to do with feeling out of place and ignored by his social peers in a rapidly changing world where he is no longer compatible.

My brother managed to avoid all of this although I'm not sure how. Truth is that we've hardly said a word to each other over the last twenty-five years or so. We simply do not know each other. He sat at the table, gazing into the distance, smoking and occasionally looking over and observing me. My father and I mostly led the conversation. He talked about life after I return and how he wants me to continue my studies.

Surprisingly, he has a copy of my book in the house that he says he'll read soon. I'll believe that when I see it, if I live that long. When I got up to leave and head home, he invited me to stay for the evening, but I declined. In hindsight I regret declining. My father is old and while we have never been close, I suddenly felt deeply regretful as I looked at the old man in front of me. He looked exhausted, full of sadness that there were so many lost years between us whilst he worked in the city and politics divided us. I am his son and he is my father. Whatever else has come between us over the years, he loves me in his own strange way.

I've always suspected that my father favoured my older siblings and that he knew I was aware of this. Honestly, it made me resent him over the years. He was never interested, he never cared about what I did, only that if I was not going to take an active role in his firm then I kept quiet and did not make a fool of myself. But looking on that evening now, I feel nothing but regret towards my relationship with my father. And I suspect he felt the same.

Staying goodbye on the doorstep, I left Hampshire and made my way back to London. It takes longer than it should do with all the transport issues and I did not get home till later. On my journey back, I had nothing but knots in my stomach. Wanting and wishing for things to be different between us. But it's too late now.

Saying farewell to Hannah was considerably worse. We both wept a lot. She tells me she will wait for me, to write to her often and to think of her when I need to find courage. She can always tell when I'm scared and now, I am truly scared. Truly frightened. I've never fired a gun at someone before, never had someone try to kill me before. Never had to stare death in the face like this. Hannah kissed me on the mouth and told me that we'd be reunited again once the war had ended – and it will end. Germany is weakened and if the war continues the way it is going it can only end in the fall of the Third Reich. She told me she will still be here and that we will continue our lives after I am home. She was always an incredible optimist.

I just do not know if I'll live to see it. We still live partially in the memory of the Great War and many more will die before this is over. I head out to France imminently. And just over the water, in a country that used to be so free, we find death and all the horrors that come with it. Hard to imagine that all which has kept us safe for so long is a channel of water.

Whenever I wrote a letter to you, I was always aware that it could be my last – that death is democratic in taking any of us at any time. But now I feel a sense of pure dread; I fear it is coming for me sooner than I realised. Morality feels like it is gripping my neck and not letting go now.

Yours my friend,

Brian

June 1944
San Francisco

Dear Sven,

Well, there is no point in being closed off about this anymore. You read the papers and I can talk to you somewhat openly of this business in France. I say business because to me I do not refer to the recent attacks on the beaches. I am instead referring to myself being denied the right to report on these events.

I had applied for a post to report on the invasion since it became knowledge to the core staff in the Chronicle. When I came to my desk the following morning, I found that my application had been returned with a firm 'denied' from my superiors. I was pretty upset about the bold, red ink on my slip and decided to muster my courage after a few cigarettes and a quick brandy and went to see my boss that morning about this.

I was not allowed to report on the invasion in France because I am a woman or so my boss claims and therefore it is dangerous to send me into such a hostile environment. Okay, I understand his logic in that this is a warzone that has been heavily occupied by the enemies of freedom who have changed Europe forever. This is not a safe job to be doing. I respect that point of view and frankly I am reluctant for any of our inexperienced journalists to take on the task.

I reminded him that I did live through World War I, unlike many of our colleagues and was therefore someone who can offer a strong perspective on the conflict. He disagreed; I am a woman, more vulnerable to harm, allegedly weaker and higher in a tendency to cull my professionalism in exchange for fear and being incapable of carrying out my job. The man insulted me by the mere suggestion that I cannot do this job on the basis of my gender.

And the long and short of this is that I am really disheartened by the outcome. I am forbidden. I cannot understand why this is not allowed, only that it reflects the world we live in; a world where men still dominate and own women and may treat them as they wish. Honestly, this is why I never married, nor had children in my life as I felt that to be a servant to a man is to submit the most basic necessities of what it means for me to call myself a woman.

True, I go to bed with men frequently enough but this for my pleasure, not for them to court me into some warped cycle of dealing with children and a house whilst he works and provides for us. I am not a servant to anyone – I live my life the way I want to do so. Alas, it appears these outdated and frankly abusive perceptions of how men treat women is something that will outlive me.

Still, I fought on for my right to go and placed an appeal against my boss last week. It was again rejected on similar merits to the previous rejection but with (meaningless from my perspective) the promise that I would be first in line for our next major project and that I would expect to be heading it. Needless to say, I no longer care. They'll probably all get killed by those fascists in Europe anyway.

But I feel...disappointed that I am considered not good enough, on the basis of my sex and not my merits as a first-class journalist, writer and scholar of the world. I hold the highest-ranking position in the company for a female and I simply do not take any crap from some of the younger, naïve staff who still hold onto family traditions that women belong in the home and not at work. I should add that this has probably only served to heighten my reputation in the company as a trouble maker. In fact, I am simply fighting for what I want to do, not what I am told to do.

I shall give you an update on the situation as things progress but I do not remain positive about the eventual outcome. I have just written this letter after reviewing the significance of Hemingway in literature over the last twenty years – seems he was allowed to go France this summer without his qualifications being contested.

I'm going to bed and sending this in the morning.

Yours,

Cassandra

June 1944
Countryside, twenty miles from Rouen

Dear Sven,

We are on the march. Taken the beaches of Normandy, hammering the Germans back, despite heavy losses.

Writing this in a rush. Safe with my unit in Northern France. Scared shitless.

Lads in my unit think my humour is hilarious. Keeps up the moral. Was not in the first attack for D-Day so managed to avoid the worst of the blood bath. Still seen enough to give you nightmares for weeks.

Much love,

Brian.

August 1944
Paris

Dear Sven,

I'm back in Paris after five years.

This city is understandably not how I remember it. It has changed and is no doubt damaged by the force of the Nazi war machine against the sword of liberalism.

I am holding up alright. It is incredible to think that we have advanced this quickly into Europe. Friends have been killed, buildings destroyed, entire towns taken off the map. I've seen allied officers rape young French girls, toy with the failing lives of German officers who they've fatally wounded, heads blown off...I have not seen everything in life but I've seen enough to know that I do not want to be here.

I keep reminding myself just why we are here. Because of us, the French capital is now back in the hands of their Republic or at least what is left of it. Walking the streets for the first time in years, I see ruined buildings and dead bodies but I see the smiles of French citizens and I hear voices of hope in the streets.

War has numbed me. I cannot confirm nor deny if I've killed men because I'm not sure. I've been shot at, screamed at...but I'm still alive. I'm not sure when I'll be writing to you again but know that in this moment I am still here. Paris has been liberated and the tide has turned against these fascist dogs. Many more will die before this is over and I genuinely believe that it can only end in the death of Hitler. He cannot go any other way and by our hands will that madman die.

I write to Hannah often. She is holding me together. I am still only a boy really. Barely a man, scared shitless by what I've seen over here. It is truly abhorrent to try describing the details to her. She is looking after our flat and I hope in my heart that I will be able to return to her someday. I need to. I have to survive this war because my burning love for her keeps me whole. It is this that gives me the will to fight on.

So I leave this letter here, written in Paris, now free of the fascists who have damaged her so gravely. Know that I am alright. I cannot deny being frightened. But the fear gives me the will to fight on. The fear of knowing that I cannot leave this world whilst Hannah is still in it.

In a few years, I hope we look back and laugh about this on some beach somewhere, smoking cigars and watching her dancing on the shoreline with your wife.

Yours my friend.

Brian

October 1944
San Francisco

Dear Sven,

I had thought I'd sent you a letter telling you about how things were over here but it seems I cannot recall so I'm going to send you another.

Dearest Sven,

So, I'm now leading a team on the writing projects for the Japanese conflict in the Pacific Ocean. A huge promotion for me – I'm now basically in charge of an entire department. Money talks and I'm paid more now than my salary in Princeton. I even feel like I enjoy this work more now, since I can boss people around again and not have to answer to anyone beyond my immediate senior.

All I really do is edit the work that the junior journalists on my staff do. It takes about four hours a day and I'm usually in the office by eight in the morning and finishing the bulk of the work just before lunch. The disadvantage to this is that it is all on me to make sure the final pieces are polished and ready for submission to the newspaper. This takes up pretty much my whole afternoon. Between that and working on my own projects, I seem to only have free time on the weekends.

But I honestly cannot complain. I feel very happy doing this right now and I do not feel like my time is wasted, although it is sparse. Living in San Francisco in a nice apartment with a well-paying job, being able to be on my own and to live life on my own terms again is where I wanted to be. I almost feel like the last several years were worth it and I keep a low profile outside of the office. I attend bars on the weekends away from the office of the Chronicle so that I can keep my personal and professional lives separate.

France must be an utter mess right now. You have not mentioned Brian to me in many years now Sven. Is he still in England or did he manage to get out of the country before war started? I'm not even sure if he is still alive. Do you have news of him? I cannot even begin to imagine all the carnage and death on the beaches of Normandy...

We've just witnessed around 60 Japanese war ships engage with our naval forces in the Pacific Ocean. This is the largest naval battle I've ever heard of, indeed it could be the greatest of all time. The Leyte Gulf is how historians will remember this...surely with all the success of the Allies and the failures of the Axis powers – you'd think they'd simply give up the ghost by now.

Anyway, nothing to report here. Be safe in Lisbon – things are real ugly in Europe right now!

Yours,

Cassandra

October 1944

Paris

Dear Sven,

Been in Paris as a stationed sentry since we retook her from the fascists. The cold is setting in now and it seems like it'll be a rough winter. We are due to be transferred back to an advancing force in two days, now that we have had a chance to gather our strength again.

Morale is good. Most of the lads are positive and we laugh, share jokes and talk about our girls back home. The French girls are really beautiful, with their accents and style of dress; many sleep with the officers. But I remain faithful to Hannah. I am hers and she is mine. That is all I have to say on the matter.

France is still shaken up by the damage caused to her but we are optimistic about the turn of the tide. I only hope that we never have to enter another war like this again. I suspect that this end to the war will be the death of Germany as we know it. We've all got blood on our hands – but our hand was forced in an act of self-defence against these aggressors.

And despite the horror and the bloodshed, I'm proud of our efforts to fight these lunatics.

Be well Sven,

Brian.

December 1944
The Rhineland

Dear Sven,

Happy Christmas my friend!

I'm writing to you from France. To tell you that in this moment, I am not part of the many dead men in the fields yet. I could have been. But I'm not. Do not worry about me right now. I am safe and sound in a farm house with my unit. We advanced for several days until we saw the house, occupied by German soldiers. Then we stormed the farm house on Christmas Eve.

They never saw us coming. The Europeans usually celebrate Christmas on the 24th and not on the 25th. We knew the Germans in the farmhouse were unprepared for a surprise attack - we were not. I was assigned the rear guard to keep any counter attacks at bay from the farm yard whilst the rest of the unit stormed the house. We entered through the front and backdoors, whilst one officer fired his Thompson machine gun through the window of the dining room. Most of them, minus a few sentries, were sat around a large table, sharing the meagre scraps of a Christmas dinner together.

We shot them all to death. Every last one of them. The bloodbath that followed will mark me for a long time to come. I took no part in the shootings but I heard the screams, saw men die. Two of our own, eight of theirs in the end. Two seriously wounded on their side, who both died shortly after. We caught them completely off guard and butchered anyone that attempted to resist. The stench of death in the air was heavy and the smell of gunfire lingered in the house long after we secured the area and lit up with the welcome relief of nicotine.

I'm not proud of being a part of this. But it is war. A long and bloody war that is coming to its conclusion. Some of these men were fathers or uncles. All were sons to someone. No one was under forty in that farm house. We feasted on the remains of the dinner to stop our ravenous hunger. Although it was poor compared to what I'd experienced in my family home, I was not ungrateful.

You'll judge me this time. I believe most men will. The people we shot were unarmed. Boys really. Kids sent away from their families to fight the war of a lunatic that is already lost. And now all of them are lying in the garden. Our commanding officer told us we'd bury them in the morning, if we had time. 'If we have time', he says. How much time do any of us have? Ten minutes before we turned up, they were probably telling jokes, talking about how they pray for their families in Germany, hoping that they were holding up in the absence of their sons.

And it might be long before the families know they are dead – even longer as to how and where their bodies might be found. We slaughtered them. Just as the Luftwaffe slaughtered our civilians in the Blitz and as our own men were cut down by the thousands on the beaches and else where. In war, there cannot be such a thing as hesitation. If the surprise attack had failed, we might all be dead instead.

Do I regret my part? I cannot say. Only that this is war - we do not have a choice any longer. It seems that we either fight and die or fight and live. I do not want to die. I did not want to come here but here I am anyway. So I made my choice. To fight and live. The same way these boys did until we cut them down. Slaughtered them like the owner of this farm once did to his livestock. In that respect we never had a choice – only a madman would choose pacifism in these times.

I was on sentry duty until 2 am. Then, on Christmas morning I was relieved from my watch by Max, a young northern lad that I have befriended in my time in France. Together we have played cards, smoked cigarettes, talked about girls and laughed about Hitler's tash. All whilst joining in on this campaign to retake Europe. I like Max. He offers a humanisation to all of this.

As I drifted off to sleep, exhausted and feeling overjoyed that I'd survived another cold day in hell, I thought only of Hannah. Where she was, who she was with for Christmas right now. How she was holding up. If she had enough food for Christmas. If she feared I was dead...

Then I woke up, almost after five hours of unbroken sleep, to think of her again, as I always do when I wake up in this hell and find that I have not been killed in the night like those kids we slaughtered on Christmas Eve.

I freely admit it Sven. If I could go back now then I would. But we cannot go back now. Only forward. With this, I tell you that I am still alive.

Happy Christmas my dear friend.

Brian

January 1945
San Francisco

Dear Sven,

It is so cold today. I never liked this time of year, be it in New York or San Francisco. The ice on the road, the fact that I require several layers of clothing to make it from my front door to the tram. Steep hills make traversing the city harder than usual. How the hell do the Swedes manage this?

I feel well and truly at home in California now. With the benefit of hindsight I have built a refreshing perspective on life. I can be who I want to be here. My friends and colleagues know that in the past I have made mistakes which devalued my career and status. But here, being paid to help spearhead a major company in the world of news – that is a fine trade from that of my teaching lifestyle. I have adjusted.

I played bridge earlier this evening, in a club a few blocks from my home. It was really great fun and although I lost outright in the game, it was really good to get out and socialize. My usual social outings, as you know, seem to be in the company of men and smoky rooms. To try something different every so often is probably what I need. The variation helps.

In news, a bill relief will be brought in at the end of the war, according to city officials, which allows for up to $40,000,000 to be spent to aid in the aftermath of the war. The thing that brought hope to me more than anything else was the phrasing of the 'aftermath of the war.' It is true that those of us on the side of liberty and democratic principles are also those on the winning side of the conflict. But to hear it – the aftermath of the war. Our light at the end of the tunnel. It is all getting better. We are finally seeing an end to what I know is the worst conflict in human history. I remind you that I lived through one world war already. To witness another in my life time is far from hopeful.

Even with all the shitty weather right now, I feel the rays of optimism creeping through the window of my apartment every morning (even though I often rise from the depths before sunrise.) The brilliance that this is not all we will exist for. War. You'll forgive me of course. San Francisco is one of the most militarized cities in America. We are surrounded by guns and ships wherever we go. Then again, I imagine Lisbon is as well.

Anyway, I've got to go out in an hour to meet a friend for a wine and a chat about her family life. I'll try and write to you again before the start of February but please be warned that I'm really busy – it might take a bit longer! Sure you understand.

Yours darling,

Cassandra

April 1945
Cologne

Dear Sven,

Quickly from me to let you know I am alright. We are in Cologne, having taken it several weeks ago from the Axis powers. On the road to Berlin, I think this war is going to end for us soon. The fighting has been hard and for each German soldier we have killed, they have returned in kind. In war men always suffer so. It was the last generation before, now it is our turn.

Tanks and armed guards line the streets. A curfew is in effect. I've been hugged by German women, spat at by others, shot at, praised, abused and admired by some. I long to return to the Roxy and drink myself into a coma like times of old but I cannot. Like it or not, we have a job to do and that job is to destroy the fascists.

Are you alright? Is Portugal still the safe haven it has been all these years? I am glad that your wife is in good health from your last letter. You do not need to worry about me. So far, so good. I will return home someday unless I'm killed by a German bullet or some mad wench that thinks I shot her husband on the beaches of Normandy. I will return to Hannah. Maybe I'll take a beer with you again before our time is done.

In other words, at the time of writing this letter I am still with you. And her.

Yours,

Brian

April 1945
San Francisco

Dear Sven,

President Roosevelt died today. No one saw this coming. An unexpected loss when we are so close to defeating the Nazi forces in Europe. The Soviets are on the doorstep in Berlin, Cologne is now in the hands of the Allies, and the tide has turned in the Pacific. And I have just finished writing the draft for what will probably be my next book.

I'm going to send you a copy once I get the opportunity. I know that with everything going on in Europe and with Portuguese neutrality, you're not likely to return to Sweden for quite sometime. I do not blame you because I wouldn't want to be near the carnage in Europe.

I said last year how I wanted to go and be on the front line, to report on the D-Day landings. But it was a flight of fantasy. I cannot imagine the horror on those beaches. I am glad to avoid first hand memories now. And with the rising blood path, the tidal waves heading towards Berlin from both the east and west, I think we're both safer where we are.

About this book. Of course, I will mention you in the acknowledgments. It is a small piece of fiction about the lives of young people growing up on the east coast of America in the 1920s. Swinging jazz culture and a time that I am old enough to look back on nostalgia. It is not a long story; it will probably be just under 200 pages. Written from a first-person perspective, it should be enough to help with the retirement fund. Unfortunately, we have to write about what people want to read, not what we want to say. Dull nature of supply and demand but there is not really any other way to do it and make money from it.

I'm interviewing Chester Himes this afternoon. I've interviewed him before in Los Angeles. Chester is releasing a new novel very soon and work want me to discuss the story with him. He borrows Richard Wright's themes of the black American. Civil rights is a long way off over here and I really think we've done a good job of reducing our fellow citizens from slaves to sub-humans. So, we'll see what he has to say when I meet up with him to discuss his book. I like Chester and I think he's offering something to white America that is long overdue.

I'm taking on and off lovers in the city. I'm still not craving anything long term. I just want to be left alone to my work and to my privacy. None of them are young these days; can't seem to pull it off anymore. I'm still quite a catch but I think the twenty something year olds alike me to being old enough to be their mothers, which in a way I am. I probably should have spent more time courting the older men with money. But the truth is I like working and waking up alone in my place and being able to do what I want. I do not need someone trying to tell me how to live my life.

So, there you have it. The war continues in the Pacific and I prefer to hide out here and get on with my work. Still a massive presence of military in San Francisco; it is like being in a danger zone without the bombs going off. Safer than Berlin or what-not but sometimes it feels just as real. I really hope that we can end this without destroying every shred of Japanese culture in the world. They are a proud and honourable people; but they are still people like you, I and the rest.

In many ways I think this war has taken something from all of us. I'm going to be very busy at work in the next week, with the transition of presidential power to Truman and the race to Berlin...I would not expect to hear from me for a while.

Yours,

Cassandra

April 1945
On the road to Berlin

Dear Sven,

Explosions everywhere. Friends and enemies shot, left, right and centre. Not just literally. Figuratively. No one is being spared from the sheer carnage of this blood path. Fascist, socialist, conservative. We're all fodder for the politicians with their mad ideas.

I killed my fourth man today. Shot him through the neck, watched him bleed out in the street of some small village near Leipzig. I took no pleasure in it. It was him or the friends I've formed in this unit. He had already killed my friend Richard. Got him in the head, sent him into the next life or the black abyss directly. Unlike Richard, this German didn't die immediately. He was crying for his mother as he bled to death.

I took his hand, held him as he died and reassured him it was going to be alright. I'm not a soldier, I'm a writer. War destroys all fragments of what is left of you. It had to be him and not me. Who was this man before someone gave him a gun and told him to fight or die? A baker? Maybe he was a teacher. Or possibly a strong supporter of Himmler and Hitler? I have no idea. Does it matter? He is dead and not coming back. I know that. I looked into his eyes and watched the life fade out of them. Funny thing, watching a man die. Even stranger knowing that you're the cause of it.

My own injuries are minor. A few bruises and bumps to name a few. I managed to get a shot off at him before he could at me. His friends were gunned down by mine. We're still here and he is not. I don't want praise for my actions but I wouldn't mind if someone knew about it. He was about your age. Could have been a father for all I know. I feel awful. But tell all of that to Richard's wife.

The fourth man I've killed. Well, directly. I suspect there are many more. Odd shots squeezed off here and there, well placed grenades and luring enemy officers out so that others can shoot them all to hell. Yeah, I think there are more than I contributed to murdering. Is that even the right word? They'd do the same to us and that is why we must fight as we do. But he was the fourth I raised my gun to and deliberately fired at with the intent to kill.

I apologise to his children and maybe someday I'll meet them, have to explain why I've rendered them fatherless. My own father was something of a jerk to me but I'd still want to kill the man who takes him from me. I was left with no choice. Richard didn't get one.

Sven, I just want to go home and play football again. Chase girls, complain about our deadlines and stay up too late. Princeton feels like a thousand years ago. War is hell and we are in it.

Yours,

Brian

May 1945
San Francisco

Dear Sven,

Well it is obvious that the war in Europe is done with. Hitler is supposedly dead, Berlin is in the hands of the allies and most of the German army has been stood down by this time. We have won. At least in Europe.

Japan remains a threat to us. I do not think this will end without one of us destroying the civilisation of the other. It seems that this is purely what men are destined to do. We cannot have peace because it is not in the nature of the Japanese society to just surrender. They have a different perspective on the world to us.

We can hope for a quick victory but I believe that extreme measures might be warranted. The thing is that we have this weird relationship with the Russians, almost a case of where our hands were forced. Winston Churchill did infamously say that the enemy of his enemy was his friend. And after that enemy is dead and gone? What then? The USSR is a huge beast; it is not as if they'll just return to Moscow once this is over with. Pretty much half of Germany will never be the same again.

I've never much cared for war. But as a journalist, it is something you end up being involved in anyway. And this conflict has been enough to rewrite everything. War has changed, society has changed, and technology has changed. Hearts and minds have changed. I'm not a political scientist but I think it is clear to everyone in the office and across the intelligence sphere that things have changed forever.

Yet right now, the war is still on. It will not end until the fall of Tokyo or something more severe, I fear. Japan is unlikely to stand down. I feel sorry for them. Unlike many of my colleagues, I do not consider them sub-human or intellectually behind the times. It is a culture and a society that is just different from ours. I'm a journalist, I deal in facts. I know that they are not an evil race. But I must be blunt; we both know this will only end with more death and slaughter. Even with the campaign in Okinawa – why do they continue to drag this out? It is literal madness.

Our focus is blurry. We need to end the war and end it quickly. We are all fatigued to limits we did not know existed. This is the lousy nature of war. But I think we have dangerously underestimated the USSR. It is not just going to disappear overnight. It is here to stay. A while ago, we had someone in the office talking about the need to work with the Russians in the coming months to build a better world. I do not think the communists are interested in that. A soviet cannot be trusted. Nor can a Russian. They are one and the same. And we're stuck with them now. The Soviet Empire has only expanded with the war and I doubt they'll leave Europe to it.

Europe has been scarred and damaged beyond recognition. The Republic of France has been torn asunder and divided; fascism is alive and well in Spain; Italy and Germany will never be the same again and I fear Eastern Europe is gone from this earth. The war has destroyed us all. No one is safe and no one will be who they want to be again.

And I fear the worst is yet to come.

Yours Sven, yours. Be safe and well in Portugal.

Cassandra

July 1945
San Francisco

Dear Sven,

We've pushed Japan back to the brink. It's becoming clear that they cannot survive the coming endgame without standing down. Of course we all know that this won't happen. The imperial power is a relic of the days of valor and glory, honor and pride. It has become clear that we, as a country, will probably have to take drastic action against the Japanese in order to end this conflict. It scares me as to what might happen. We just reclaimed the Philippines – when is this going to end?

The war in Europe has been over for almost three months. The continent is in ruins. I don't even know if I dare visit the place. London has basically, after the last six years, been turned into a pile of rubble. This whole war, bloodshed, death and slaughter to stop fascism from taking over civilization...and my greatest fear - that we've overlooked a more monstrous enemy than Germany. Russia.

I'm going to bed. I don't sleep too well right now. Most of my time I look out across Golden Gate Park at night and fear the worst. I see a world of rubble, decay and doom. I sometimes don't want to wake up in that type of world. I'd rather die first. Writing this, I'm borderline black out drunk. I went to a bar after work with some friends. Have to be up in five hours to go to work...I might call in sick but at this stage I'm not sure if I can do that. Used up too many sick days of late.

Anyway, as a species we're fucked.

Cassandra

July 1945
French hospital in Paris

Dearest Sven,

I'm still alive. Oh god I am still alive. We have not conversed since April. I'll explain why. First of all, know that I am in good health, although it was a struggle. If I told you the amount of times I nearly died in this God forsaken war to destroy the thing that would only do the same to us in return; you'd die several times over of shock.

After I sent you my last letter about my fourth man, we were ambushed. Shot at by a German tank. The hulking beast crept up on us as we marched through a field. It was up on the hill. Before we had a chance...well this is the thing – we never had one. But before we could act, it was already firing at us. Mud, dirt, shrapnel and blood all mixed into one cocktail of death and flames. I saw several of my friends, men I'd served with since D-Day, blown apart. Killed then and there.

I was lucky. I avoided the worst of the carnage. I managed to drag three of my comrades into safety, underneath some bushes. Not enough to protect you from a Panzerkampfwagen IV but just enough to hide from the bastard. One of them died moments after I got him out of the firing line. He never had a chance. Guts and intestines all over the place. Screaming for God, oh screaming for someone beyond me to help him. William, he held the blokes hand as we watched him pass on. Poor fucker. He was twenty-one. Twenty fucking one. Just a kid, like we were once.

I went back. I couldn't leave them. Could you, knowing that beast of death was going to kill people who'd die for you if the situation was reversed? We are a team. Soldiers do not leave their men to die. But I'm not a soldier. Just a brave idiot with a gun. Trying to do the right thing. I got four more of them to safety before it fired again.

The whole world went black; I cannot remember anything after that.

When I woke up, I was on a stretcher. Nurses and doctors all around me. One of my friends, holding my hand, saying 'hang in there Brian.' I blacked out again. When I woke up from my death like state, I realised what had happened. My commanding officer standing over me. He'd been coming back and fourth for a few days when he could to check on the wounded.

So I'll tell you what happened Sven. I saved six men that day. Seven if you count that poor kid. God knows I tried. If not for my actions, they'd have been all killed. I might have too. I had been gravely injured. A bit of wood had been flung in my direction, smacked me on the head, took me down and sent me packing. One of the lads managed to drag me into the bushes before any further harm could be done. They checked my vitals, found a pulse and kept me alive. A counter strike from one of our planes took out the tank. Or so I'm told.

I've been in this hospital ever since. Hitler is dead. The war in Europe is over. Now the real work beings, rebuilding the continent. Saving it from fascism and communism alike. I just want to go home. Hannah never gave up on me but in our last letter she told me she'd been inconsolable. They got a telegram to her in London once they knew I was going to pull through. Told them everything. When I finally had the strength to stand and to feed myself again, I wrote to her. Assured her I am coming home. And I will. I have had enough of this. Seen enough blood and death to last a lifetime.

I'm something of a local legend in the hospital. Everyone tells me how brave I am, how it was a self-sacrificing act to try and save as many of the men as possible. I did not do it for bravery or medals or so someone can write my name in the history books thirty years from now. And I didn't do it to get killed. I did it because what else could I do? I could not just leave them to die out there.

As soon as I am able to, I will be sent home. Honourably discharged after being wounded in the line of duty. I just want a quiet life in England. Somewhere in the countryside where I can write books, drink wine in a small garden and laugh with Hannah over stupid things that no one else could understand. I just want that. I've had enough of the rest. I'm focusing all my energies on getting home and starting my life again. She's waiting for me in England and I'm not staying here any longer than I have to. Our work of liberating Germany is done. Let the politicians sort this mess out now. I want my life back.

Don't you worry about me Sven. I'm on the mend and soon I shall be home to her.

Yours old chap,

Brian.

August 1945
San Francisco

Dear Sven

The obnoxious bombings of the cities of Hiroshima and Nagasaki are something I did not know our species was capable of achieving.

Madness. Anarchy. Slaughter.

I don't know if I want to be an American today. I am not sure if I can be a part of the human race. If humanism stood for anything then I am afraid it no longer exists.

Millions of civilians have been exterminated by an atomic bomb which has fire-bombed an entire city. Whatever damage that is not caused in the initial impact and may continue to haunt Japan in later years remains to be seen. I do not know. It all seems so bleak. So barren. So empty.

The war has fuelled countless advancements in our civilisation over the last six years. But if this is what it will culminate into, the death and destruction of so many, through the mushroom clouds of the coming storm then I fear for our species and for all of whom we encounter.

Hope is a hard thing to spot in the stormy night's sky as I sit over my view of the Golden Gate Park tonight. I am fearful of what I can see. The entire races, beings, civilization. Wiped out in a matter of seconds. Lost into the ash heap of history. It does not make sense. I do not believe this ever will. No narrative can be provided for what we as representatives of humanity have done.

I cannot sleep tonight. I do not know if I will sleep again without hearing a thousand screams racing across the night's sky. The echo of death is haunting us all.

Yours my friend,

Cassandra

August 1945
London

Dear Sven,

I'm home again. Oh home, I am finally home.

My flat in London was destroyed as you know. Or maybe you don't? It was hit in a bombing attack...V2 missile or so I'm told. Hannah was luckily out at the time. We found a place to rent in Chelsea so we're living there for now. Well actually she found it but hey ho, we're not homeless which is good.

How can I describe being back? I've been home for about a week. Readjusting is hard. Hannah has been amazing in taking care of me. The streets of London are messy. I have nightmares. But I'm safe in her arms.

Labour are in power; the city is recovering and we're moving on in life. The war is done. Life may begin again. I'm going to marry that girl. She just doesn't know it yet.

Yours my friend,

Brian

October 1945
San Francisco

Dear Sven,

I found his book.

Brian's book.

It was an astonishing coincidence to be honest. A series of papers were on my desk recently and I came across a memo asking to do this book...of all the things it was his. It was published almost two years ago it seems. I have to admit that I am impressed – he often talked about this idea but he struck me as delusional in how he wanted to create his art. Like he was a dreamer.

Odd, given that he uses his real name. How I missed it I'm not sure. It appears to be something of a sleeper hit, growing in popularity since it was published. I do not believe I shall read the book for now; the memory of him still haunts my mind and the final days of Princeton. I hurt him badly, but he hurt me in the long term and ultimately caused more damage to me in the end. Something must have happened for him to actually work at it and make it happen. Let me tell you as a novelist, it is far from easy to get from the first draft to publication. After then you get criticism for it and not everyone likes it.

I rarely talk to you about Brian. The fact is that I prefer not to. Our affair cost me my job, although I still have no idea how the university became aware of it. It seems to me that he was probably the cause of it, although there is no evidence to actually support that. There is a lot I could say on him that I will not as you know why but I really do not want to read it yet. Our actions cost me my career and there is much shame and regret in the past we share. I have come to understand that my actions were indefensible and dealing with my past is not something I want to focus on for the immediate future.

I really wanted to avoid this. He had always claimed to me that he would publish a novel that would be recognised in the world. In some ways I have wondered if I would ever come across it. I thought that by accident I would find it in some second-hand book store in a seaside town populated by old people on some idle day in the fall. And now it follows my career and stalks me to the other side of the country, right on my desk as if it wants to remind me of my past.

So, I passed the job on to one of our junior journalists. Liam, a young Irish immigrant, is a fan of literature so I am sure he can manage to write a good review on the book. I have asked for it to be returned to me once he has finished his work. I intend to keep it on my shelf in case the time ever arises where I might wish to read it. For now, that will be the way it stays.

Younger generations seem interested in attacking the older ones and I wonder if he makes these claims in his novel. I did the same to a certain extent in Souls of New York but my own narrative was about the changing landscape between the young and the old whilst trying to reconcile the differences. Nowadays we see plenty of writers criticising the norm but this is honestly nothing new. There are just different styles of attacking the social norm but ever since Daniel Defoe wrote *Robinson Crusoe* this has been what the novelist is meant to do.

I do not regret assigning the job to Liam and I am looking forward to my own projects to come. The time for now is the present and the near future, not the past. Just tell me if you think he has mentioned me in the novel. That is all I really need to know. I have not spoken to him since we all left Princeton – I know you both talk but the situation was different for you.

Please do not take what I say about him unkindly. He is not a bad man I am sure. Not if you are still his friend.

Anyway, my own book is now out and ready to read in bookstores everywhere. It was published this morning.

My love to your family,

Cassandra

October 1945
London

Dearest Sven,

I'm in love with Hannah. I wanted to be with her. I saw in her hope. A woman that represents so much good in the world. She is what all those other girls could never be. I recall how I had to leave to fight and the distress it caused both of us. How I said I'd come back to her once the war was over. How she'd wait for me.

When I went back to France to fight in the war, I saw a country torn to shreds and covered with the blood of men, woman and children. The horrors of the war are things I'm still making sense of. I can't put it into words for you. Just that there was nothing left of the great country. The country side was not what I recall when I visited France all those years ago. I could still speak French, from my days in Indochina (or is it Vietnam now?), so I was able to communicate with citizens and soldiers alike. The stories I heard from them keep me up at night. The monster - the Nazi war machine, a legacy that will linger long after I'm dead and gone. Paris was not the same, scarred and damaged compared to my visit when I returned from Indochina

I'm a drug addict. I'm a published novelist. I'm a war hero (I saved six fellow soldiers from a tank in Normandy.) I'm a former womaniser. I'm a traumatised man, who doesn't know what the fuck he wants anymore. I'm completely lost and I don't know how to get back to where I came from. I don't think even know if I want to be alive now. The things we've done as a species and the harm we've caused to each other. I'm...

Sven, my reason for writing this letter to you is to only share tragic news.

Hannah was killed crossing the street by a car about three weeks after I came home in August. She was 31. She loved me and she waited through hell, fire and despair for me to return. Other than Cassandra, Hannah was the only woman I have loved. My light has gone out in the world.

Yesterday was her funeral. It was a somber affair, beautiful and full of loved ones. Even Roger was there, although we did not speak and I suspect he mourns her in his own way. Friends, colleagues. Even my father came, although he barely said a word to anyone apart from me and disappeared as soon as he could.

I feel nothing but a great emptiness. Emptiness because the one I love, who survived waiting for me while I was at risk of dying everyday, was killed in the heyday of her life. Those bright blue eyes that held so much hope in the world are closed and will never open again. I am lost without her and do not know what to do.

Indeed, after all of those near misses in France and Germany, only to come home to this, when by rights we ought to have died together in our bed of old age. It is purely and simply – not fucking fair. I go to bed tonight, alone and without meaning in the world because the one I love is gone forever.

Brian.

November 1945
San Francisco

Dear Sven,

I went for coffee with a friend this morning after giving a presentation on our weekly project at work. The topic is going to be on novels concerning the French Revolution. My friend is someone who lives to the north of San Francisco by Sacramento.

We returned to my apartment later on that day where we had sex and then we took a walk into Golden Gate Park. He stayed for the evening then left the following morning to go to a business meeting by Union Square. He flies home later in the evening. We simply fuck from time to time. I like him but I do not think he wants anything long term. A pity – I actually want a man for a change.

I decided that I should pursue this type of thing for a while as it has been simply ages since I had any sort of release. Although it has only been a short while since I wrote to you and although I am copping well in my life, I feel as if we have lost some touch. I cannot say I know where you are right now or how you have managed to cope since the end the Second World War. I can tell you that I am perplexed, tired and no longer enchanted by the wonders of my country. The blood on our hands after the last six years seems appropriately mirrored by the color staring back on our flags.

I do not care about the cause against these Axis Powers any more. Only about rebuilding the world. In Berlin, we face a new enemy. Bolshevik ideology now Communism. The most profound threat in the known world against capitalism. Away with fascism, we now have another monster to fight, another beast to slay so we can justify our own right to live and exist. This whole thing sickens me – when do we call it a day and stop murdering each other? The bodies in Hiroshima and Nagasaki are still smoldering and we now want to divert our attention to fight these idealists in the east of Europe. The human race needs to stop and breathe before anyone else gets sent to the slaughter house.

I do not offer any hope to the human race after August 1945 and I am yet to step away from that cynicism, even now.

I understand from your last letter that you are going to head back to Sweden soon. How lovely that you are now able to do so. I know that you were effectively marooned in Portugal since the outbreak of the war. I am happy for you, darling Sven.

Yours,

Cassandra

December 1945
London

Dear Sven,

I almost shot myself yesterday night. Well, this morning actually. I don't know. It has been a disturbing blur of emotions and whiskey that have reduced me to a shivering wreck of a man. I don't actually feel like a man at all right now.

When I close my eyes, I only see the face of Hannah. I see her smiling at me across the table; I see her dancing in Hyde Park; holding my hand when I need comfort. And now she is a rotting corpse. Dead and rotting in the ground. Never coming back.

Like so many of the kids I saw butchered on the beaches of Normandy, the children of a generation, shot to bits like the poor bastards we were fighting against who serve the same sinister imperial bastards as us. Just this time last year, I helped slaughter a group of young soldiers in a farm house in the name of liberty.

So, I went for my revolver. I kept it as a memento when I was discharged from the army. It sits in a cardboard box in my closet. I felt the grip of the handle in my hand. I opened my mouth and placed the metal barrel in my mouth. I cocked the hammer of the revolver and waited.

And I waited. I don't know how long I sat there for, gun in my mouth...my eyes were closed and I just waited for my fingers to muster the courage.

I saw her. I saw her as I remembered her. I miss her. Oh god I miss her. The idea that I must wake up tomorrow and go without seeing her, do the same thing the next day…the day after. Until the day I die. I see the faces of the boys who died on the beaches. The lad, no older than 19, Jack, whose hand I held as he died in the sand and blood. He'd been hit in the gut by shrapnel and was bleeding out. In shock. Crying for his mother, like all the others did. The faces of all those lads and old boys, massacred on the beaches. Had I have known that I would live through this; I wish I'd died with them.

I can always blow my brains out tomorrow morning. But I know I won't. I promise you that. I'm too cowardly to do it. I'm brave enough to rescue men from death and risk being blown into bits of flesh and bone but I'm not brave enough to admit when my life is failing and shoot myself dead. I cannot do it.

But I cannot do this either. I am terminally depressed. Life is pointless. London is too painful. There was a time when I once loved this city. But that was then. That was before Hannah was broken into bits and reduced to nothing more than a lifeless body. That was before I returned to a home I no longer recognise. As you know our flat was destroyed in a V2 Rocket attack whilst I was on the march of death to Berlin.

She wasn't there then. She was out. Why did she survive the war, only to be butchered in the fashion that she was? There is no God who could exist that would subject me to this living hell. We had hope after I got back alive. Readjusting to real life was hard enough. Doing this without her is near impossible.

Fuck it all. And fuck it all some more.

I'm skipping work today and going to the pub to get drunk. Don't worry about me old chap; I won't do anything stupid. I'm not going to shoot myself over grief. No matter the temptation.

Yours my lifeline,

Brian

PART IV

January 1946
London

Dear Sven,

I apologise for giving you the impression that I wanted to kill myself. I do not mean to concern you; only that I needed time to grieve. To come to terms with the situation of Hannah not being here.

After Hannah's funeral, I fell into a period of intense depression. I'm still in it now. I get up in the mornings, I go to work, I come home, I sleep then I repeat the exercise. I struggle to keep my head above everything else. I cannot say that I'm not looked after. Friends and colleagues have taken me to their homes and into pubs after work to make sure that I am not alone.

But I am a mess inside. I try to be brave and to get through it, but if I'm honest, I have barely kept my head above water since the day she died. It was the final curtain in my life. I went through a cycle of where I constantly debated if life was worth living - if I should kill myself. But I have not. I managed to pull through, even if I almost did not. It has been almost impossible to cope.

I have got through the worst of it; I no longer have suicidal thoughts or at least not as much. I see horror in my dreams and I see it in the day to day of life. To further explain why I feel the way I do, it is simple. I went through war, death, slaughter and see all of that in my mind. Then I saw her die in front of me. I cannot hold it against the driver of the car. I have seen true murder in my life and I have seen accidents. This was an accident.

So, it was no more than an act of God. An act of God! Ha! God deserted us all in Europe when all those lads got shot to death on the beaches in Normandy or the many that were murdered in

Germany...I just do not know my friend. God left me the day my mother died. That is all I can really say on this. Bertrand Russell put it better than I ever could about why I am not a Christian.

I will continue on for now but I am directionless. My glazed eyes, my hat and coat whilst walking to work, blending in with many of the other office drones; I cannot write and I cannot think. I have lost the best part of me. I know that this is almost unrecoverable. I feel like I am lost.

But I believe I am starting to slowly recover. It is like attempting to rewrite your life after having everything meaningful stripped away. But it can be done. Greater men than I have had worse. But it is a relative thing – I do not know how this could be worse.

I miss her everyday. And I always will. Sven, do not worry about me. Despite the horror I am rightly painting in this letter – I have no intentions of taking my own life over this.

Brian.

March 1946
Hastings

Dear Sven,

I am still surviving.

How are you my friend? Probably better than me. Christmas was okay. Never really told you about it. I spent it with some friends who live in Hastings. They moved out here from London after their son was killed in the V2 attack in May. I knew the boy – Dennis. Lovely young lad. After everything we have all suffered, his parents Leonard and June needed someone to share their pain. I needed the same thing.

I spent most of the Christmas break walking the beaches, talking with them about life. We shared laughs, drank wine and ate freshly caught fish that June acquired from the local fisherman. Walks on the sea front, discussing ideas about writers and occasionally bursting into tears about our loved ones. At least we can all cry about it. I suppose this is better than bottling the feelings up inside.

I will tell you that despite all the effort, it has been a lousy Christmas. But when I think about the carnage, I saw in France last year; I have to remind myself that it could be so much worse. But that seems hard to relate to when the woman you love is dead and buried.

Sven, have a wonderful Christmas.

Brian.

July 1946
Hampshire

Dear Sven,

I have spent the last month or so with the old man. His health is declining and it is obvious to even the blind. I have attended his house every weekend for the last six weeks, talking with him about life and what my plans are. Indeed, it is funny in a strange sense. Since Hannah died, my father and I have become closer, oddly enough. He was widowed when I was eight years old. That was twenty-three years ago.

We hardly spoke a word to each other which contained any meaning from the day mother died to the last year or so. After I was sent to the front, we shared a moment that filled us both with recognition. Recognition for the wasted years of regret that passed where we barely knew each other at all. And now we attempt to make up for lost time as his health declines.

My siblings are seldom seen. Clive, the asshole that he is, saw me two weeks ago on the terrace of my fathers' home and barely said a word to me. My sister has not seen me, bar once since I came home from the front. They are both meaningless to me and the feeling is mutual. My father is not the case. He spoke to me recently for the first time, with fondness of my mother and their early days together. He even showed what I believe were faint signs of a smile at one point when he told me about their first year of starting the law firm together.

Once, the other week, he spoke to me about my book. He said that he did not understand what I was attempting to do in my story, but that he had at least read it and thought it was a good book. He was even able to talk to me about the characters in the story and how it ended. That he was impressed by it, although he admitted that he only read it because I wrote it.

This might not sound like much but coming from my father, this is high praise. In the last few weeks, I feel that something has changed between my old man and I. That instead of us just being connected by blood, that we almost respect each other now and that conversations are of mutual interest. He even asked me if I planned to write a second book.

We spoke of Hannah and my mother often. This is the most open I have seen the old man in years, if not ever. He told me that he was sorry about my loss, asked me how I was coping. That I needed direction, even though I am directionless. Then he removed his spectacles, looked me directly in the eyes, with his own grey eyes and told me that no matter how hard we try, we never truly get over their loss. That life will move on, but we, as people, do not forget.

He sat back in his chair as he always did after making a sincere point and took a sip of whiskey. In the sunshine on that particular afternoon, my father looked old. Really old. But he smiled at me for the first time in years adding that despite this, it allows us to grow as men. He advised me to change firms, telling me that I needed new focus in my life. That I have to keep going. So, I have decided to apply to a different company.

This time with my father has offered a strange catharsis for me. In that I seem to have some clarity about where I should be focusing on my life and that it could take years to deal with the loss of Hannah. But that maybe I can soften the damage to my heart and mind. I also feel like I have started to bond with the old man. He is still my father, despite all that we have been through.

And I feel like I have been offered a sagacious perspective. That I must not spend my days being angry and full of sadness, like he openly admitted to me in our conversations. He gave me the impression that he has lived a life full of regret, even though he did not openly say this. My father has offered me a lifeline through his comments. That I must not make the same mistakes as him; to learn from him.

So, I am going to start looking around for a new firm. Instead of being a journalist for a magazine, I believe it might be time to start looking at editing. To help others with their work – although I want to continue with mine at some point.

Anyway Sven, I'm very far from alright. My father is aging beyond his years whilst I mourn my lost love. But I think I might be starting to feel okay. The old empire is dying and I do not want to die with it. I can either go and live my life or stay here and slowly rot with the rest of the country. I have to take action and reclaim my life.

I feel...changed. Like there could be a glimmer of hope after all.

Take care old chap,

Brian.

November 1946
London

Dear Sven,

I've been working in this firm for the last month whilst I try to readjust to society. Seems to be proving impossible. I struggle to get out of bed. When I sleep, I have nightmares. Of the city burning in the Blitz, hiding in the mud in France and avoiding death with that tank attack by the skin of my teeth. The sound of planes flying near and talk of the advancement into Paris...then I dream of her when I am both awake and asleep.

Missing her. It has been over a year since Hannah died.

I'm recovering, slowly and not without bumps in the road. It is not easy.

Because I am deeply disturbed by the things I have seen. I can openly admit this to you. It is too early to make sense of things. In London it is business as usual. We still have the stiff British upper lip, the mentality of just getting on with things. Rationing is to continue for now, no idea for how long. I cycle to work because I cannot bear the idea of having to be stuffed into the tube. Even when it snows; I feel caged, like a rat waiting for the end.

What is becoming clear is that I cannot remain in this country. I need to leave. There is nothing for me now. All I can see when I have my eyes closed is the ruined landscape of France. The carnage and blood all in front of me as if it is happening all over again, like it is a constant day of despair and death that repeats itself.

And when I keep my eyes open all I can see is her face in the rain.

I am working in this new firm as an editor. I was taken on because of my experience as a journalist and my book. I am actually slowly working on my second one right now, although progress is difficult. Yesterday I put in for a transfer to our office in Cape Town, South Africa. This is going to be a fresh start for me – an attempt to move on with my life. I've been back here for over a year and it has been an emotional fist-fight to stay alive. If I am going to continue living my life then I will no longer do it in England. The empire is decaying and I will not die with it.

My transfer should be confirmed by the New Year. The firm will provide the expenses for me to move and to get started in an apartment. Once I am set up, I will attempt to start a new life. My old life died with Hannah – there was enough left of me after coming home for her to help rebuild me. But now, it seems I can only do it myself.

So that is it. My father has accepted the transfer warmly, since he believes that I am correct in my view point that my life needs to perk up. He believes that South Africa might be a place for me to start, claiming it to be up and coming in the world. I just want to go somewhere very different from the old country. Europe is too badly damaged – there are many a great memories here that I do not want to deal with. Not yet. Maybe not ever. You might call it running away. I call it survival.

I want you to know that I am making this decision from what I have seen in the last three years. Love, death, war and peace. I have had enough. I need a new start. I am desperate for it. I think this will help me cope.

You take care Sven. I hope the move to Sweden went well. I know you moved for similar reasons to me in the end – we both needed to start again.

Anyway - I leave in four months, directly after February.

Yours,

Brian.

March 1947
Cape Town, South Africa

Dear Sven,

I arrived in Cape Town two weeks ago. Moved into my one-bedroom apartment in the city centre; it's a five-minute walk to work. I've come here to escape. To escape the nightmares of the war and to forget that Hannah is dead and not coming back. I see her in my dreams; constantly smiling at me, then the moment comes. The car that struck her down, took her life away from her…

Fuck it, I had to stop for a minute because I just burst into tears at the thought of that. I cannot write anymore about her today. I am in bits.

I'll try to tell you about South Africa instead. Well, its bloody hot here. Even for March. I guess I'm not used to it. Living in Europe for too long. Everyone in the office seems nice enough but they're adjusting to the new guy; their boss. I'm in charge of an entire editing department. I have the air of mystery about me. Rumours are like wild fire. The war hero. The novelist. The quiet guy who does not talk too much but doesn't keep as silent as the grave.

A few of the staff had read my book. I can't say I was shocked. The thing has become something of a recent craze in the writing world. Having the war attached to your name makes people admire you in a strange sort of way. They don't look at you as some kid from Hampshire; instead they look at you as a man of the world. This seems to be the way I've grown as a person; oblivious to these things because I'm too down in my own despair.

All in all, I'm not sure if I like it here. I guess I'll adapt in time. Finding my feet. I haven't been out of the city much. I tend to go out with my work colleagues and I've signed up for a literacy club that meets every Tuesday night. For now, I'm just seeing how it all goes.

Cape Town is dangerous. Really dangerous. The negroes have basically no rights here. They're treated like a subspecies. Actually, it is a fair comment to say that unless you are white, then best of luck getting by. There are about ten different languages but you only really hear Afrikaans or English. I've started learning Afrikaans but everyone in the office speaks English. It's a legal requirement.

Time will tell how all of this goes. I'll write to you again soon.

Brian

May 1947
San Francisco

Dear Sven,

How lovely to hear from you after so long. You'll forgive me for not writing to you in the last year or so; I have been working on so many projects that I have not had the time to even stop and see friends, let alone write to them. Excuses all around, please accept my apologies.

Thank you for telling me that you've relocated back to Stockholm. I cannot believe that it has been ten years since we last saw each other in person yet we continue to write to each other after all this time. The world is a funny place. Of course, I shall attempt to come to Stockholm at some point if I can. Getting time off is a pain but I'll see what I can do

In your letter, you say that you have moved back because the war is now over and you believe it to be safe for your children to return to their country of origin. I'm glad you feel this way. Too many are now refugees in Europe and the continent is divided. It shall never look the same again. My own experiences of Europe cease after the 1920s. I do long to wander the streets of Paris and Amsterdam again. I'm just not sure what I'll find.

Not much to report here. Just finished interviewing John Steinbeck about his new novella, The Pearl. All about family, good and evil and corruption. As a family man, maybe you should check it out sometime. I think its up your street.

I'm feeling calmer these days. I do not drink as much but I continue to drink and smoke, work long hours and sleep little. I keep up the party lifestyle and my second book has demanded that I produce a third. I think it shall be a follow up, partly in themes with the first book I published five years ago. Yes, I think it is time to address those stories again. Enough time has past and I believe I am in a position to write it now. I could not have done it so long ago but now I want to. I just have no idea how to start it off.

Maybe you can offer me some perspective on that? I trust your judgement and opinion on how to craft a good story, since you've heard so many of mine. No new man in my life as I wish to predictably keep it. I don't really have as much casual sex as I used to, although I picked up this handsome thirty-five-year-old last week for my pleasure. I won't be seeing him again. I don't want to.

Sven, tell me more about your family life and what it is that gives you such joy in your next letter. Write to me when you can with all your news. Of course, I shall not use you directly in the next book; you may sleep peacefully at night over that.

Yours my friend, I wish you a pleasant time as you live in Sweden with your family.

Cassandra

May 1947
Cape Town

Dear Sven,

It's been two years since the war in Europe came to an end.
Yet I'm still breathing the dust from the aftermath of the Blitz,
still shaking off the tremors I felt from the explosions in
Normandy as we took the beach from the Germans. Sometimes I
wake up in cold sweats after dreaming of these horrors. If I close
my eyes, I can see bodies burning in the distance. Screaming and
shaking, the sound of cracking skin and hair against flames. I see
nothing past that - only a black emptiness. Just death and silence.

I see dead children, women and men in my dreams. The
carnage of the war has led me to realize that win or lose, no one
gets out of this without being damaged. I've never seen death on
such a furious scale. I'd never thought I'd live to see a time when
mankind exists solely to build machines of war to rid each other
from the face of the earth. One thing is certain after all of this -
that none of us will ever reach heaven after the monstrous
actions we've committed.

You might think that I'm callous in these remarks. That the
Nazi's deserved to be taken off the map, nay, had to be stopped.
Yes, they had to be otherwise our actions would have been all for
nothing. No longer could we justly call ourselves human beings if
we did not stand up to these demons whom have destroyed an
entire culture of civilization. The monsters came out of Berlin to
crush the world, the world fought back and won. It was the right
thing to do. The only thing left to do.

So, we went back to Germany after twenty-six years and
brought the Nazi's to their knees. But was the price worth it?
How did we fall so far in trying to undo this power? We fought

the beast but I lost myself in the process. I no longer know who I am or what I try to be in my life. I only see dead memories. Those who I loved who fell by the wayside. I've only ever been used. Used by my teachers for academic points and sexual favours, left behind by those I really care about because death strikes in the heart of those you truly love regardless of how well you steel yourself against it. That none of us are ever safe, at any point and that we will all be gone from the earth before we know it. Yes, I lost myself. Whatever hope I had left of humanity was burnt from my mind and heart.

I hope that I can start to change that now.

I shall devote my next novel to Hannah and my past. Then I will move forward and build a new identity.

Yours my friend. I hope your life is full of happiness and love.

Brian

August 1947
Cape Town

Dear Sven,

Well I've done it. I have completed the first draft of my new book. I have spent the last four months trying and failing to come up with a consistent plot. Yet with everything going on in the political landscape of South Africa, along with my own demons and the work I'm doing – it has taken time. But I'm happy to tell you that I finally have something.

I'll send you the draft in due course. I have to be happy with the edits and rewrites before I decided to go any further. You know what writers are like – strange folk. I've adjusted to living in Cape Town. I do not know how long I'll stay here. The pay is good, the company covers the cost of my flat and I am in high demand in the office. People like me and it seems that I get on well with everyone.

But this country is in a political transition; that much is for certain. It is not safe walking the streets alone at night and aggression towards foreigners is high to say the least. Some are not welcome and others are full of hatred towards the negro. But little of this seems to affect me directly as I am allowed to flourish in the office.

When I told my team that my side project was completing my second book, well everyone became very excited. Many of them get on with me and liked the first book. I'm considered something of a local legend in the editing world down here. Like a man who has experienced the world. In reality, I feel as little more than a youngster, made into what he is by circumstances and if I could change a lot of it then I would.

Standing in the living room of my apartment, smoking a cigarette and looking at the half-drunk bottle of whiskey on the coffee table, I think about what my life has become. Ten years ago, I was setting out to go to Indochina. Now I find myself here, in Cape Town. Another place on the eve of political transformation. I have a habit of throwing myself into places that are constantly in these situations and I think it satisfies a disturbed craving in my psyche.

Often, I stay at home and read books or work on my articles. I have become something of a recluse in the last couple of years. Ultimately, I put this down to living a life without my darling Hannah. I intend to dedicate my next novel to her memory and she serves as the primary inspiration. I've taken a journalistic, almost Hemingway style of writing to this story; making it as real as possible about a man who goes to war, only for his wife to perish whilst he is gone. He returns and attempts to deal with his life. I've set the story in World War I to allow for a bit of poetic license.

Really this is my attempt at healing myself by writing about it. I've concluded that this might be the only way to deal with her loss. Her memory haunts me as I sleep and when I close my eyes in the day, I can see her face. Those beautiful blue eyes and the blonde Danish hair...the smile and if I am feeling particularly melancholy, well then, I can sometimes hear her laughter. My memory of her, although only a memory and not reality, feels incredibly real to me. Writing about it is painful but I struggle to talk about her to anyone. So, writing to you my friend, is the best form of catharsis for me.

It is hilarious, in a sort of painfully ironic manner. If I spoke to the man, I was ten years ago and told him I had made it as a journalist, a published author and held a senior editing position in a company that pays for my apartment; that man would be over the moon with joy. As it happens, my life feels incredibly empty. There are few things I find joy in these days. I feel self-destructive and argumentative. I drink constantly and do so often on my lunch breaks. I am openly disgusted with how people in this country treat others.

I am an angry man. And I believe I will only become worse with age. Like a cheap beer, instead of a fine wine. Cassandra felt like a drop in the ocean compared to the gravity of Hannah's loss.

Sven, I wish you all the best this summer and hope that you and the family are well.

Yours,

Brian.

=

=

August 1947
Los Angeles

Dear Sven,

Taken some days off to visit Los Angeles to see a friend. I'm pretty tired, having been working flat out lately on both my book and at the office. It feels like I have not really slept properly all month and now what I want is to just rest. In many ways the work load is the same it has always been. Long days sitting at desks and drafting up notes or in cafes with friends or interviewing people that the Chronicle wants to talk to. It seems to go on and on, yet I feel constantly worn thin.

I just got promoted to deputy head of the department of editing in the Chronicle. I've earned this and it has raised my salary to an amount where I can work four days a week without worrying over money. Works for me – more time on my books. I'd say I fought for this position actually over men who are dry, old and out of touch with the world. My skills as a writer and an academic have given me an edge over these people. I'm the only woman who holds such a high-ranking position in the Chronicle and I created a persona of not being someone to dismiss in an idle fashion.

I'm getting fat. I'm an older woman now, this much is for certain but I am getting fat. I've always been small framed, taken care of myself with healthy choices and protected myself from the Californian weather. But I cannot deny that the aging process is starting to creep up. I had trouble getting out of bed the other day; hence why I am here right now. I just needed a break. I'm out of the office until Thursday morning. It is now a Sunday and we are lazing about my friend's house in Los Angeles today, doing very little other than taking time off, smoking cigarettes and eating lots of food.

My friend, Ben is from a farm in Utah, having moved here directly after university. He now teaches at an acting school. In some ways, I'm envious of his low-profile job and the fact that his time off is his own. In other ways, I feel cheery that I am a woman of a distinguished newspaper, working in the centre of a city that has soul and a warm vibe.

But back on my health; despite the weight gain, I feel like I am worn thin and constantly fatigued from the last few weeks. Being here and taking time off from everything helps me recharge my batteries and my mind. I am again not working the weekend after I return to San Francisco so it is not too awful. Everything lately has been a challenge but I am confident that I will rise to the occasion.

And how is your new born? I imagine this must be quite a world changer for you, being a father and all. Ah, you've called her Tamsin? An usually contemporary name (that I naturally approve of) for a Swedish and Portuguese couple but it has a lovely ring to it. Tell me all about your life in your next letter.

I'll be in touch over the next few weeks about the status of my book. I intend to send you a signed copy of it once it is finished.

Cassandra

October 1947
San Francisco

Dear Sven,

I decided to go to Union Square for lunch, to meet with my publishing agent about the novel I've decided to write. I chain smoked through the lunch, not really talking to my agent, who seemed to be blabbering on about the nature of book sales in New York. He's a nice guy; that much is certain, although I don't really care for him beyond getting what I need from him.

I've been offered a solid deal for my next novel, which I accepted directly. What I failed to mention is that I do not have any idea what I'm going to write. I haven't even some lousy first draft to work with. All my previous drafts were scrapped by moi.

What do I say? How do I invent an imaginary character from scratch? My mind is blocked from all the drink and drugs I've consumed. I see nothing fantastic in the world anymore other than the drudgery of modernism. Nothing excites me and I've destroyed my own imagination. But I haven't destroyed my past. Nor have I exactly dealt with it. I make no apologies for who I am or what I have done in the past. I am simply another person trying to make sense of this hopeless hole called Earth. That's all I really have left to say. I'm too fucking old to care anymore.

The other day I discussed this with Raymond Chandler, who I spent an afternoon interviewing for the Chronicle. He was actually very encouraging turning these thoughts to paper and this makes me believe that I have an opportunity here. When I read your last letter, from the summer, I felt good about how you praised my ability as a writer. I think this is my opportunity to write a really good follow up to Souls of New York in a similar fashion.

Love to you and the family,

Cassandra

November 1947
Cape Town

Dear Sven,

I have finished the drafts. The rewrites are done. The novel is going to be published in the early spring, once I get the final pieces sorted and talk to a few people. I edited the novel myself, with two other men I work with in our department. My colleague, Mark, has been amazing in getting me to finish the book. Twice I almost gave up, yet he convinced me to keep going, to say what I needed to say in the novel.

Standing at four-hundred pages, I think I can safely say this is the finest thing I have ever created. It has even pulled me from being a recluse to actually attending lectures at the local university on the nature of the novel in the modern age. I gave three lectures over the last two months on the relationship between the novel and modernity.

Mark has been fantastic in promoting this through his contacts. He runs an art business that buys and sells works of the last forty years. His specialty in the subject knows no limit and he has been extremely helpful in promoting my book through his trade. This is in addition to being an editor on the board at our company. We spent several weeks, over drinks in our local café, going over the work and he offered an uncompromising honesty about how to create the story into what it is.

So I made a point of thanking him in the novel's acknowledgements. I also put you in there for encouraging me to complete the story and for all your support. A few others who have been helping me along the way. I make a point of mentioning that my studies at Princeton helped shape my understanding of the world around me. Along with my father for simply being my father.

I spoke to the old man recently. He reached out to me, to tell me that he wishes me well and that he is proud of me. I've finally won his respect. At the tail end of his life. Well, better late than never. I remain single by choice, although not celibate. I have returned to my antics of sleeping with women, although I keep it to seedy bars and it is for my needs only. In some respects, I'm transitioning to the role that Cassandra once had with me, except I am now her in that regard.

I hope she is alright, although I have well and truly forgotten her, except for when I occasionally talk with you. Our office occasionally deals with the Chronicle in San Francisco, although I have not communicated with her at all – indeed I'm not even sure if she is still in that line of work. Please do not tell her that I've mentioned her though. Some things are best left alone.

So, I have it done now. Cape Town continues to disgust me and I find that the more time I spend in the growing limelight, the more I object to this place and its growing racism. Talk of the National Party winning the election next year is growing. I dislike those fascist dogs intensely. I saw it in Europe and what it does to people. My left-wing view point, shared by Mark and others in our office makes us unnecessary targets of our enemies. I do not fear for my safety yet. But I am aware that it could come to that.

In the mean time, thank you for helping me with this book Sven. We have not seen each other in years but the strength of our bond through the letters we continue to exchange makes me realise that I've always had a friend in you.

I'll be in touch and if we do not converse before Christmas then enjoy yours.

Brian.

January 1948
San Francisco

Dear Sven,

I've been taken ill - seriously ill, actually.

Spent the last four days in a ward in the hospital in San Francisco. It seems I have a chest infection and there were shadows found on my lungs. My doctor has advised me to lay off the cigarettes and booze; for me this is like having a death sentence. But it might be that I'm overdue for one.

I found myself in bed one morning with this stranger I'd gone home with the night before. Well it was actually an afternoon in late December...and I was unable to breathe. Literally unable to breathe, like my lungs were filled with cement. I could not move, managing with considerable effort to speak, I was able to tell him that I was not well. I think he figured it out because an ambulance turned up at the front door twenty minutes later.

Was it a stroke or something? Not sure but it was serious. I felt like I was struggling at every turn – it was impossible to make sense of anything real. I was rushed to hospital and kept in the ward for those four days where the doctors told me I was lucky to be alive. I've passed the point of no return. I am seriously ill and this has been something of a wake-up call. Taken time off work to recover and try to get things back on track.

I decided to not tell you initially because I did not want you to worry and because what could you do anyway? You could offer me sympathy and tell me you want the best for my health. Beyond that, how can well wishing help someone with health as lousy as mine? Medical science is the only thing that can save oneself in these situations – you can forget about anything else being effective.

Even now I am sorry to have to tell you about this. With everything going on in our lives right now and the growing gap between us because of how we are getting older. I'm probably causing you unnecessary worry. Please know that the doctors have told me that I'm expected to make a full recovery, providing that I am careful with my health.

On a more positive point, I've started writing the early stages of my third novel. So far, all I have are a few chapters and some notes. I successfully began the thing about five days before I became ill and although I intend to return to it soon, the work has been stalled over my bout of poor health. Nevertheless, the work shall continue, for I need something to keep me going. Writing fiction has become something that helps me identify my relationship with others and gives me a sharper focus on the past since I can alter certain details about the past for mine own benefit.

Perhaps the best thing about it is that I do not have to admit that it is me, Cassandra, who is discussing her own past but the lives of fictional people. Doing this whilst addressing the past we share seems to be the best way to be open about it without being revealing. Do you understand what I mean when I talk about a person's relationship between literature and their past? I hope you might because it seems to be the best method I can find for healing.

Anyway, please do not feel concern for me. It has been a rough week but I'm starting to recover now and the doctors have dismissed this as anything beyond a serious chest infection. I have decided to take a few weeks off work and allow myself time to recover. I might decide to visit the parks in Eastern California to give myself some much-needed peace of mind in this compacted city.

I do not mean to scare you Sven. I just wanted you to know that things have been difficult for me lately.

Be well and be happy darling.

Cassandra

March 1948
Cape Town

Dear Sven,

I've been in this place for too long already. It is really a stinking hole of racism. General elections are up in May and frankly I stand corrected; the bastards in the NP are going to get in. The African National Congress does not have a leg to stand on. Also does not help that they're pretty Marxist and no one likes the reds these days.

But the racism disgusts me. I'm personally not the biggest fan of the Indians in London but I've got no axe to grind with them. The flood of immigration since the war ended is huge. Things are tense in this town. So, tense you could cut it with a knife.

The other night I was in a bar. I heard these three white men talking about blacks being socially inferior to whites. But not just your typical run of the mill racism that I've seen in England about Indians and Pakistanis. I mean, violent, hateful and almost murderous. Sinister and greedy, disgusting and vile forms. Colonialism and its legacy is far from dead in this country. What the hell am I doing here?

After a while, I became pretty disgusted about this rot and approached the men. The journalist in me created this and I openly accept responsibility for my actions. I started by offering to buy the men a drink. They asked when I spoke if I was from out of town. Answer; no, I live here. Although I do not think I want to anymore. I'm blind with remorse for Hannah when I'm stinking drunk and, in this case, I was full of aggression. Aggression for this kind of disgusting behaviour.

You see, I fought along side blacks in the war. We fought and died together. In those moments, when you look to the man next to you, there is nothing more than that. Just a man. Like all others. The same desire to live, the same desire to protect his fellow soldiers and the same desire to be back in the arms of his loved one. And they fought bravely against the beast of fascism. I did not come here to experience this shit again – I came here to start my life over.

After a few minutes of tense conversation, in which I spoke about these experiences, one of them made a comment that caused me to snap. Looking me directly in the eyes, this square jawed racist said to me 'you sound like one of them nigger lovers.' And that was it. One of my colleagues had to pull me off of the man; I smashed my shot glass as hard as I could into his face. Screaming, he went down on the ground. His allies leap to his defence and we ended up fighting.

I've never been an aggressive man. Well, not until the war. That was when it all changed, and I saw things that'll make you different. Things that are impossible to in France. His gun had jammed; I was armed only with my blade. We fought for a while, then I cut him badly. After this, he went down, and I quickly put him out of his misery. Judging by how he looked, I would have said he was my age.

So, in many ways these punks never knew what was coming. Truth be told, I went over there because I wanted to start a fight with them. My colleague got involved in my defence and we went at it with them. In the end, one left with a broken nose and a dislocated arm. The other was coughing up blood from where I'd tried to ram a piece of broken glass into his chest. The third went to the hospital. I don't regret it – I regret not killing them.

But now I fear I am a marked man. Those men were rich, white, and Afrikaans. Not the sort of gentlemen you want to rough up unless you're prepared to deal with the consequences. Friends in town with power, that sort of thing. But to make it clear, I'm not scared of them at all. I simply do not like them. It felt good. Really good to hurt them like that. But I fear they might act against me in kind. I am on my guard now and I still own my service weapon from the war. I always travel with it now.

Sven do not fret about my safety. Take it from me – the bastards had it coming to them. Just a waste of whiskey going into the first man's eye. But it made it more painful for him. And I feel good about that. I might have to get out of South Africa. I fear that I've cooked my goose with these people and that it is simply better to leave before anymore trouble starts. I do not want to leave the job. I actually really like it and if not for the scummy Afrikaans in town I might reconsider.

Except there is no more opportunity to reconsider.

Sven, I want you to know that if something happens to me, if I don't reply to you after this letter is sent, then you might know that this was it. But don't count me out just yet.

Yours my friend,

Brian

April 1948
San Francisco

Dear Sven,

I have had to postpone work on my book. My health is, as you know, taking a turn for the worst right now. I've had the last few weeks in and out of work, mostly as part time but on full time benefits whilst I combat my illness.

I constantly feel tired and worn out. Like it is a great effort to summon the will to rise from bed in the morning, get on a tram and go out. Even my usual pastime of smoking whilst listening to jazz music is difficult to do; I quickly lose concentration and struggle with staying lucid.

In moments like this I cannot deny feeling truly alone. It allows for good reflection of my life and how I have decided to live it these past forty years. I often feel like I have lived a morally corrupt life and got away with it. Well, got away with it in the sense of landing on my feet and being able to move to the next thing without having any major setbacks.

I broke it off with some guy I was with a few months before I became sick. Turns out he had a wife and two children living in Los Angeles. This sort of crap I could do without. I will not resign to being a second rate, secret mistress who is only seen on business trips and otherwise kept under the rug. I didn't really like him anyway. He was 40, balding and did not smoke. He'd also never read Nietzsche or Camus. I mean, be serious about life if you're going to work in the literature field and do not ignore titans that will last long after we're all dead.

But the ignorance of literature in this person never really concerned me. I've slept with plenty of people who preferred math and psychics to novels. It was being treated as second best. I have a long and profound career as a journalist and a lecturer. With more qualifications than half of the office, I know what I am and I know what I am not.

I deserve better than his behaviour. But maybe, despite the solid career in journalism, the reputation I managed to secure after being effectively placed into exile from the academic world...well just maybe the career was not too important. Maybe all the drinking, fucking, all the running and not always doing it on stable ground is responsible for this.

Maybe this is my punishment for breaking away from my very conservative upbringing. My family never really supported the start of my career in literature, except for my father. He was able to secure my first job as a part time lecturer in New York whilst I expanded my career. But I had a reputation for being a socialite and he hated it. But because I was so damn good at my work, I held enough respect to be recognised.

Looking back now, I think he was proud of me. It was his support that allowed me to continue in the field. Few challenged him. The mighty professor of his field, holding down an enormous salary and constantly being away at conferences and seminars. My mother was an extremely devout Roman Catholic. He was not. They married for circumstances I'll never understand. I learnt from him. Including how to break up relationships and get what I want.

By the time he finally left her in the spring of 1933 I had been at Princeton for a year. He died seven months later when he fell down the grand staircase of his sparsely populated six-bedroom house. She left the world two years later. I did not attend her funeral.

And now I might be dying here. I have not been able to smoke a cigarette in five hours, owing to the coughing fit I had in the night. Still, I'll smoke again. I still hate myself enough; not to see the folly in my ways.

Yours,

Cassandra

July 1948
San Francisco

Dear Sven,

I submitted the draft for my third novel last week. The thing has been incredibly challenging to write and at one stage I almost gave up. It has required revisiting parts of my past that I'm yet to completely deal with. My past is corrupt and harsh. I've used many people. I've abused the system and I have lied to many people. Never to you though.

So, I've changed names in this story and I've altered certain facts because they were simply too graphic for the published word. But everything else is pretty much correct down to the detail. It tells the story of what happens when you screw your life up and have to restart of the other side of the country. I've told you all of this information because I know you will probably come across the novel at some stage - you're bound to, given that we still talk ten years later.

Don't judge me too harshly for the way I've portrayed some of the people we both used to know. It isn't an attack on them - this novel is my way of trying to live with my mistakes. Atonement if you will. I don't know how else to do so. At my age, it is time for me to accept responsibility for my actions by placing my story into literature. I have to accept that I have made numerous mistakes for the actions.

This novel is my way of dealing with my past. So, names and times are changed but otherwise the story deals with all of these issues. My issues, yours, theirs...so let's be honest. The only one on trial here is me. I've escaped the past so far. It is time to deal with it. I've told my agent, the press, and other writers that this is about Californian students. But this is a lie. It is about my past at

Princeton and the corrupt bitch that I once was. I have to publish the story. It tells you what you need to know – but caution my friend – it is the things I do not say that are concerning. Stories that I don't deal with are things in my past that I cannot yet confront. They might surface in the rewriting – I'm not sure.

Why am I telling you this? Because you are one of the few people who might realize that I am not entirely screwed up. We often exchange letters of friendship and decency. I know that of all those in my past, you were one of the few who simply accepted me for who I was. That I could just be me around you. That was of course, how Brian came into the sphere and how the death knell of my career was sounded. To be honest, I used him. He was in love. I can't blame him for what happened. His outcome in the novel is fair and redeemable. Read the book for details on the antagonist Sven.

The novel is meant to be set in the first person detailing three characters at university and their decline. Except the story takes place in different universe. It has nothing to do with Princeton. The story deals with students different from any I knew. But it is basically about the three of us. I have come to accept that in my past I have been a monster. This was the hardest thing I've ever had to put to written word. But now it's becoming a reality.

I never intend to tell anyone else what this story is about. It has nothing to do with anything but I know that you have a right to know about this. It is about our time in Princeton. And how we lived.

For the prose and rambles of this dull letter; I can only apologise. Writing is much a much harder thing these days.

Cass

August 1948
Cape Town

Dear Sven,

It is clear that I am drinking too much. And fighting too much. I have so much aggression. I feel the urge to harm others that I dislike. I'm losing it badly at this point. The NP has taken hold in South Africa; their disgusting racism in denial is at hand in the country. It seems that those guys I beat up in the bar are connected to this party and thus I have made an unfortunate name for myself as a man who creates problems.

I never leave the flat in Cape Town without my service weapon. I only go out to work and to buy food and cigarettes. The city is becoming absolutely intolerable and I do not wish to stay here for a great deal longer. I fear for my safety. I am known in the office for being a bit of a street fighter; with my history in the war and my knowledge of books. I do not want to live in a country that democratically votes for this type of segregation. I live in paranoia that I might disappear or be killed by these thugs whilst I leave for work.

Sven, I'm going to move to New York. The time has come to return to America. There is nothing for me in England anymore; Vietnam is no longer safe to go back to with the revolution; Europe is too badly damaged; America it is. Safest place for me despite the bad memories.

I have finished my second book. You'll find a copy in this letter. I won't say anymore on it for now – you can tell me what you think of it.

How are things now that you're settled in Sweden? I miss you and I intend to see you soon. Oh, all of my friends from the days of Princeton, you are the only one that has bothered to be in touch consistently. For that you have my utmost respect for maintaining our friendship.

I will let you know when I leave for New York. I've decided since writing this that I am leaving. And leaving within a month. I am in total fear of how this country will go. I wanted to start a new life here but it has become impossible. I am damaged by Hannah no longer being here. She's rotting in the ground, her body in London. I could not bear to stay there; every time I think of her, I'm torn between depression and anger. Depression that I lost her; anger that after being shot at by a tank and saving comrades from certain death; I only came home to have her taken from me.

I'll let you know when I arrive in New York. I have to get out of here. It is no longer safe to be here.

Yours my friend, always thinking of you,

Brian.

December 1948
San Francisco

Dearest Sven,

Let me start by saying God Jul! The children must be lucid by now that Father Christmas is probably coming to visit them soon. I wish you and your family another wonderful year of joy.

I am still in the process of rewriting the book. It is taking time but you asked for progress so I call this progress. I have not been rushing my work because I have taken longer than I wanted but probably needed to recover. But it is still happening and I'm going to be the best I can with it.

Not much else to report. My job is going alright. I've had to suspend a lot of the work on my book in order to catch up in the office. I'm not as young as I once was and trying to work at the level I used to work at; on multiple projects at once with minimal sleep and hangovers that I could once shake off in five minutes no longer seems to be the business of the day. It would seem the aging process is catching up to me, like Joyce with his sight. Such is life.

I have been feeling lousy lately but to be honest, I never felt like I properly recovered from the chest infection in January. I was ill to the point of where I felt like things were stripped from me. I remain positive but I feel fatigued pretty frequently. I have lost a part of me, something that does not remain that once was. I have trouble sleeping and when I do, it is a light sleep, like I am unable to successfully rest.

Old age, you might ask? No; poor health. I struggle to do things like I used to. I've done it to myself. Too many smokes, too many cocktails – not enough rest and being healthy. I'm floundering in the wake of all these new journalists we have recruited. I still hold the respect that I have commanded in the majority of my tenure at the office. But I frankly loathe all of these new recruits. What is worse is that some of them favour the company of the same sex exclusively. A practice I do not approve of. Not natural or normal for certain. A man was not intended to sleep only with men – the same can be said of a woman. I don't have a problem with it. I actually don't really care. But the intolerance of my opinion on the matter is what disgusts me – justifiably I believe.

This coupled with bad tempers and failing health has made me difficult to be around. Not that I ever required their approval anyway. But I certainly earn the reputation of being a bitch. I deserve their contempt because I differ from their deviating ways. It is not trendy or acceptable for me to possess such tunnel vision about the world for the new generation.

I believe that my illness and coming decline is a symptom of the post-war environment that we live in. Where everyone is starting to come to a divide about America's place in the world and our responsibilities to others. A world in that we were eager to inherit beyond the carnage in Europe. Yet it has caused me immense fatigue and a lack of enthusiasm in the world. And to a certain extent a lack of power in that I cannot seem to see past the basics, owing to my struggles with being able to work at my favoured pace. Therefore, I believe that like Russia once was, I am in turn the sick woman in America.

Too conservative for people half my age, too liberal for people who I knew that are now dead and gone. Stein spoke of this as a symptom of being lost. 'A Lost Generation' – that's the term she used. I am not lost; I am disconnected from the world and as I contemplate my mortality in this life, I see a similarity between what Stein claimed and something else. I am not strictly speaking becoming lost. I am becoming irrelevant in an otherwise changing world that I believe I no longer understand.

And it is a life that will prove to have little meaning once I am gone.

But not you Sven. Because you are a good father and you have people who love you and that you love in return. Your memory will last. Mine will fade because there is no one left to love me. No legacy for me to leave behind; save one – my writings.

This is why I endeavour to finish my novel and do it quickly. If I could, then maybe the time should come to leave San Francisco for other pastures. I have been here for ten years and now I tire, like the old woman I am who stares death in the distant face as he gazes across the fields of France.

But death is a tale for another time. For now, I am alright. I can linger in this world for now, even if I struggle to identify with the younger generation.

Have a wonderful Christmas Sven,

Your friend,

Cassandra

April 1949
San Francisco

Dear Sven,

I attended the opening night for my book last night. The most successful thing I've written so far – the reception has been profoundly positive. My reputation as a writer has come late in my life but I am overjoyed that it has finally come. All the sins of the past seem to be washed away somewhat. Well what I mean is that I have built a legacy that I think I can be proud of. A shame my father is not alive to see it.

Win or lose in life, this is my finest hour. There is talk of my book becoming a best seller in New York. Published under my true name, it offers a sparse yet direct follow up to Souls of New York. This is art and I am becoming a master in my field. Better than all the other dullards in the city.

Several famous writers attended the release and all praised the work of the story. Critics have called it the best book of the year so far. I cannot be ungrateful for that because it is the best book of the year. Because I wrote it. No one else could have achieved what I set out to achieve in the story. I learnt to be economic with my writing and ensure that every word served a purpose.

When you craft what I can craft then you know you are a genius. It just takes time for that to be recognised by the masses but recognition is finally mine. I believe that if this book steers its course then I can probably retire from the Chronicle and solely work as an author of fiction. I should have taken this path years ago. Should have skipped all the pain of being a woman in a man's world and just told them all what I really think behind the mask of being a novelist.

I want to continue writing my books and step down from journalism. I believe this might be possible at last with the coming of my next book that I intend to publish at the end of next year. A writer never runs out of things to say when the life that has been lived is one like mine.

My health is still shaky and this is why I'd like to resign from journalism within the next two years. I want to continue to be a successful writer but my desire to work in journalism has completely left me because I see the fruits in writing a decent couple of books. Building that reputation means that I am expected to write better books each time and I cannot do this whilst I work in the Chronicle. It taught me how to go from a clunky academic style to a refined and sparse style where every word counts.

So we will see what happens but I've made up my mind. Two years from now I want to relocate and go to an area where my books can flourish. Maybe the Caribbean. Somewhere that will allow me to maintain my creative mind and focus. I think it might be better for my aging body too. My health has continued to concern me and I still act like I'm fifteen years younger than I am. It will catch up with me.

My creative genius aside; you were instrumental in helping me get this book done. Last year was very taxing on my health and I want you to know this would have never happened without a Swedish civil servant so far from California.

All my love to you,

Cassandra

June 1949
San Francisco

Dear Sven,

You say you've had no word from Brian in over a year? You almost never mention him in your letters to me. And I never think to ask. But since you raised him first with me, then I will answer you. You say he published a second book? I might yet read it someday.

But honestly Sven, I must remind you that from the end of 1945 to mid 1947, we did not converse at all. Things got in the way. Life, work, sex, drugs and the reminder that life is fucked up. Do not worry about Brian. I'm sure you'll find that he is fine and simply swamped with work. I believe I am correct there and that he'll turn up sooner than later.

Something I did not say to you was that we, the Chronicle, reviewed his first book in a paper about two years ago. Okay, I told you I was aware of its existence but that was about it. Well, I did read it in the end and I have to say that I was proud to call myself his tutor, although I have never told anyone about the book; save you.

He deserved better than what he got but I imagine he is absolutely fine. He probably just lost your address. Maybe telegram his company and ask where he went if he is not there anymore? I doubt he stuck around in South Africa, with the Apartheid and the state sanctioned racism that makes the deep south look pleasant to live in. He probably went back to Europe.

Be reassured Sven. I imagine he is fine.

Cassandra

August 1949
San Francisco

Dear Sven,

I know you started talking to me about Brian again because you're concerned for him. I want you to know I would be concerned too. But my focus is else where.

I'm dying Sven.

I mean we are all dying inside from the harshness of life and trying to not gain mortal wounds from our past actions in life as we limp from place to place.

But I'm dying of cancer.

I became ill about two weeks ago. I was walking up Russian Hill. I had planned to stop at the top of the hill, take in the view of Alcatraz Island and then go down the hill and into the wharf. Did you know that from Hyde Street you can get a great view of the bay? It was just there that I suddenly had an intense pain in my body unlike any other that I had experienced before in my life. It's what I've come to imagine childbirth to be like…

Falling, crashing, passing out, I woke up in a hospital bed. St Luke's Cancer Clinic actually. I'd be there for about three days, semi-conscious. I'd been in hospital earlier last year. That chest infection? I thought it was a recurrence of that. But I was wrong.

I was released two days ago. From what I'm told, it's terminal.

I've stopped smoking cigarettes and drinking alcohol but I'm afraid that won't make a blind bit of difference now. I'll go back to them soon, I think. What is the fucking point when its this late in the day?

I wanted to leave San Francisco and I'd actually engineered a plan outside of wishful thinking to resign from the Chronicle in the spring next year and move to Paris. None of that is going to happen now. Too little, too late.

I've started writing a will; I've set out some instructions to people in the event of my impending death. All that is left now is to wait for the coming end. Or not. I don't know yet. I might have one last rattle with my life before the final sunset. But know that I'm dying. I've been dying my whole life. But now the moment of when this will happen is in sight.

Do I feel differently? I don't know. In truth I've been dying of the same amoral behaviour for the last forty years. Only now, I can see the grim reaper, staring back at me in the mirror.

Cassandra

September 1949
San Francisco

Dear Sven,

Why do I continue to do it to myself? I am drinking like the world is coming to an end. Started smoking again and continuing to destroy my liver. My health is failing me. I have been going to the hospital on and off lately. The doctors tell me that it is definitely an aggressive cancer; I'll be a lucky woman if I live another five years.

Treatment is limited. I have several bouts of illness in the last year. As we discussed in our recent letters, the cancer came calling in the summer. There are indeed bad days and then there are worse days. The most regrettable thing of dealing with this feels like the fact that I brought this on myself. Everyone knows drinking, smoking and living a rackety lifestyle can encourage rather than discourage these things. But I kept going on, like it was my fix that helped me get through the goddamn day. And now it seems, this is the very thing that'll kill me.

I do fear, very genuinely, that this will stop me from writing. From creating my art and giving me the freedom to express myself. I suppose I'm glad it was not a heart attack or a stroke; that would be a clear-cut sign of my lifestyle being rejected by my body. At least cancer is as old as the dinosaurs and that I'm dying of something pretty predictable, like most people I knew. The fear of preventing me from writing exists. I often wonder if it is a psychological aliment rather than a physical one. Here I am writing to you after being afraid of this very thing. I can still do it – I'm just not sure if I think I can.

This is a curious illness to be dying from. Well, we're dying each and everyday; born into a losing struggle. 'Man is born free, and everywhere he is in chains', to cite Rousseau. But some of us are dying faster it seems. Medical drugs for this procedure are near on impossible and primitive. In some circles or so I hear, mustard gas from the Great War is used.

I have had to sit in the hospital and have bouts of medication forced upon me. I feel weakened and depleted after each session; I do not believe it is helping me. I almost preferred not having to deal with it in this manner and instead going without. But I have to try and put my trust in medical science.

Writing this has been exhausting but I will finish. I have been forced to suspend working at the Chronicle for now because I simply cannot manage it. I am constantly fatigued and in pain. My focus is blurry and I struggle to make a cup of coffee in the mornings right now. I miss my routine and long to go back to it but my doctors inform me it'll only cause more damage at this stage.

Yours Sven. I am dying alright.

Cassandra

March 1950
San Francisco

Dear Sven,

This morning I woke up from my sleep in my hospital bed. I can hardly call it sleep – the pain in my left side is becoming unbearable. I find that it has been getting considerably worse over the last few days...I've been in and out of hospital over the last year. I told you I was dying about six months ago from lung cancer. I was correct in that assumption...it has been exhausting just being alive over this period of time.

I moved into the hospital about a month ago, pretty much for good. I haven't moved out of my apartment, not officially. And I'm on long term sick leave from my job at the Chronicle. But I feel like I resigned the moment mortality started looking me in the face. Well, it has been staring me in the face since I can recall my first memories. But now I'm feeling the fingertips of Death wrapping around my throat.

My doctor is meant to visit me this afternoon. Another dose of chemicals to try and keep the cancer at bay whilst simultaneously offering another death sentence from the men in the white coats. They seem pretty interested to talk to me, with one of the doctors asking if I could sign his copy of my book. I feel like this has a lot less to do with genuine interest in my work and considerably more with antiques and missed opportunities. I guess a signed copy of a book is worth a lot more once the author is dead. Maybe he'll tell his children that he met me and what a grumpy bitch I am? Or maybe he'll give them the book as some gleaming inspiration for them in later life.

I was able to attend a book signing about nine months ago in which I met a lot of people who wanted to know where the inspiration for the younger man in the novel came from. I told them it was about a boy I grew up with in school who later became a civil rights leader. I told others that it was about someone I used to play bridge with on Sunday afternoons instead of watching baseball. I told someone else that I did not know and I just make the answers up as they come to me. But I did not tell them the truth...my fiction is intended to mask and atone for my past together.

We both know it was Brian I was writing about.

Our lives are simple and in the scheme of things there are no great mysteries in life. Only the adventure of being what we are. A copy of some book lies by the side of my desk. I've never heard of the author nor the book. No clue when it was published. I'm meant to be an expert in literature even though I left my post at Princeton over ten years ago. But the colleague who dropped the book off reminded me when I asked who the hell the author was that this was not the question to be asking. My colleague said that that once he published it, he left a mark on the world. That this author and I were of the same breed. We leave our mark on the world and that this is where it counts. He told me I'd like the book after his friend read it.

I'm glad I'm dying in this city. Back when I moved here, I fucking hated being here. I'm sure you recall the rants in my letters, the disgust of living in this place. But that changed and New York lost its charm each time I revisited it in my memories. I became increasingly more at home and felt that this city on the western coast was where I belonged. When I knew that my life had started to fade, it became clear: I'd stay here and die in peace.

My visitors are mostly colleagues from work, quite a few fans, and my lawyer. I hate the last guy but I needed to rewrite a bit of my will. I'm ensuring that some of my royalties go to the hospital for their care for cancer patients in the city. Otherwise I've not really had anyone visit. I've been dying for some time and the news wears off after a while. My parents have been dead for years...no siblings...the aunt passed away in 1940...ten years ago now. I enjoy spending a lot of my time with the fans. They at least want to talk about my next book...which won't be happening now.

That last bit depresses me. Knowing that I won't be doing any more books. Alas, this is the way the world works. Regret is a nasty thing. So is writing this letter but the payoff is in the act of telling you where I am and what I'm doing. I do not ask you to come to the city to visit me. My condition has worsened considerably in the last few days, taking me by surprise. You were always noble in telling me I'd outlast this cancer but it dies with me and I am dying. It is like an obscene parody of being with child – hosting another life but with the opposite of birth. The only birth that follows its concept is the birth of tragedy. Nietzsche echoes in my mind as I write this.

Do not come to see me in this sorry state. Remember me as I was, not what I have become.

I haven't written a word for the last three hours in this letter to you. I had to stop because the effort was causing fatigue and then I had a conversation with the doctor who is in charge of my care. He tells me another few months but I suspect it is less than that. He is prepared to discharge me later in the week to return home...but I know that I won't be going home. Not this time. I recall the many walks in the Golden Gate Park and how I first moved to that district, what feels like a lifetime ago now. I'll never walk in that park again. I'll never drink coffee in the shops by Union Square and listen to the music of the city whilst I read my book...I'll never look into your eyes again.

I'm going to try and read some of this book later on that has been by my bedside table all morning. I've finally looked over at the name of the author. It has clicked. It was his book. I know it. The drugs are creating confusion in my brain. The second one that he wrote about his lover. I have no idea why I even want to read it. But I think it is only fair that I look back into the past one final time and revisit the man I once knew. I'm glad he finally put his thoughts to paper. He was awfully gifted and something of an underdog. I think that is what attracted me to him in the beginning, all those years ago, on the other side of the country, when we were young and healthy and I wanted him to discover his potential. I had believed when he was gone that I had ruined his love of literature.

It seems I was mistaken. Good. I've always enjoyed surprises. But I'm afraid there are none left for me. Give it a week or two and you'll be reading no more letters from me.

A final rasp of death and then...

And then nothing.

Yours, always my friend. See you on the other side.

Cassandra

Epilogue

March 1950 was the last time I ever spoke with Cassandra. Her obituary appeared in a copy of the San Francisco Chronicle the following month, confirming that she had died several days after writing her final letter to me.

When Cassandra died, it was a disaster. She had actively courted death through her bohemian lifestyle and made no bones about it in her final letters to me. I don't know if Brian mourned her - if he was even still with us. Cassandra was, as the British say, like marmite; you either loved her or hated her. In my case, I adored her. We'd spend many hours conversing through our letters, putting the world to rights about issues that were afoot in the world. And we trusted each other.

Brian was well aware that I kept in touch with her but as we agreed, never discussed her openly in our exchanges - it was always too much for him. By the time I'd read her final letter, Cassandra had already died of the cancer that ravaged her body. There was nothing I could do but mourn for her loss. I never blamed her for things with Brian. Truth be known, they were both good people that made questionable decisions.

But in the end both of them were the same; fundamentally human after all.

I never spoke to Brian again. I do not know if he made it to New York. I do not know if he simply lost my address but this is unlikely. I do not know if he was murdered by others or if he shot himself. In the days of writing this novel, I suspect that he did not disappear on his own terms. I do not believe he would have killed himself.

But this is only my own suspicion.

I later hired an investigator to find out what happened to him. There was no trace of him after this letter. We do not know what happened to him or why. I suspect his warnings and fears in his final letters were well founded; he was not a man who lived in fear without justification. I contacted his father, with my concerns about him and we attempted to find Brian. We simply do not know what happened. The old man died heart broken and alone in 1956, never knowing the truth. In his final exchange with me, he revealed that Brian was, in the end, the favourite of his children.

In putting him in this novel, I want you to know that there was such a man as Brian. He was rash and short-sighted. He had a temper to him and in his earlier days, a lust for women and affection. He was also a war hero who saved the lives of six men one day in Germany from a tank that ruthlessly shot his comrades down. He wrote several novels, loved a woman who he gave everything to and she was taken from his life too soon. He had a roaring laugh to him that all recognised in Princeton. Well read and even better liked, he had a career as a journalist in a time when that profession meant something. And he was a good friend of mine.

Whatever happened to him, this novel is intended to remember him as the man I knew.

The last thoughts of his father still haunt me to the day I day and reminds me that we must always tell people we care about them. I've tried to do that in this novel by telling the world the story of my two friends; Brian and Cassandra.

I'm seventy-seven now. My children have grown up and left home. I'm widowed but at peace with this. Unlike Brian and Hannah, I had a long and happy marriage. Spending all of my time in Stockholm and doing very little else, maybe my life is not to the example set out by Brian and Cassandra. Indeed, the creation of this story is about the only thing of note that I've accomplished since I left Portugal. And it is their story really, not mine.

It is told to remember them. You might find Brian sympathetic; you might loathe Cassandra. That is for you to decide. And you might also decide on whether Cassandra redeemed herself as a person as I have decided. And you might never give up hope in the back of your mind, even on some rainy day when you are lambasted with paperwork, commuting home from your dull office job for the weekend that Brian was okay in the end. I have never gave up hope on him.

After I lost them, my life suddenly became less meaningful, even though I had everything to be grateful for in my life. This novel is an attempt to keep their memories alive; lest they die with me.

Please remember them for what they were in this novel, that never deviated too far from the truth - they were my friends and are not to be judged too harshly. After all, they at least tried to do the right thing in life; to be good people.

Acknowledgements

I would like to thank everyone who read this book, gave me feedback on it, picked up a copy of it on their commute to work or simply bought it

It is my pleasure to share this story with you. Again, thank you.

For those personally, I would like to thank my immediate family for their encouragement and support.

For my partner, Marine, who encouraged me to complete this novel and for supporting me in finishing what I started. And for her encouraging words - 'you have no business calling yourself a writer until you actually publish something.'

Thank you to Liam, Ben, Mark, Ross, Jordan, Jack, Durga, Paul, Max, and Madison.

A thank you to the Tessier family of Bordeaux and their respective partners.

A special thank you to Tamsin - the first person to be aware of the book since it is conception.

And most of all, thank you to my mother Sally for your guidance and support during this project.

About the Author

Charles Andrews is a British author, living and working in South East England.

Author of 'Letters From Abroad' and 'The Soldier Side' (Coming 2020.

Printed in Great Britain
by Amazon